VAN  RY
DE P9-CFC-090

THE
SUBSTITUTE
BRIDE

THE SUBSTITUTE BRIDE

•

Carol Hutchens

AVALON BOOKS
NEW YORK

Hut

© Copyright 2006 by Carol Hutchens
All rights reserved.
All the characters in this book are fictitious,
and any resemblance to actual persons,
living or dead, is purely coincidental.
Published by Thomas Bouregy & Co., Inc.
160 Madison Avenue, New York, NY 10016

Library of Congress Cataloging-in-Publication Data

Hutchens, Carol.
The substitute bride / Carol Hutchens.
p. cm.
ISBN 0-8034-9793-8 (acid-free paper)
1. Women dressmakers—Fiction. 2. Weddings—Fiction. I. Title.

PS3608.U858S83 2006
813'.6—dc22   2006008517

PRINTED IN THE UNITED STATES OF AMERICA
ON ACID-FREE PAPER
BY HADDON CRAFTSMEN, BLOOMSBURG, PENNSYLVANIA

7/06
journey

To my parents, for teaching us to work for our goals.

To my husband Larry and sons Aaron and Stan, for their encouragement and support. I love you!

To Erin Cartwright Niumata. Many thanks for giving me this opportunity.

To Valerie Parv for writing *The Art of Romance Writing*, and for always being there to answer our questions.

To Holly Jacobs and Sierra Donovan for kind words of encouragement.

To Miss Jones, who taught me to sew, which formed a good basis for writing: if you don't get it right the first time, rip it out and start over.

And to the members of The Castle. May your dreams come true.

Chapter One

Think like a real bride!

Emiline Anastasia Gray took a final sashaying step as the wedding march ended and stopped beside a man bearing a startling likeness to a movie star currently making tabloid news. Shivers of excitement swished the designer gown against her legs. The whisper of luxurious fabrics reminded Ellie why she had agreed to take part in this fake wedding, why she had risked everything to come to New York City in the sweltering heat of August.

"Dearly beloved . . ."

Hundreds of guests filled the sanctuary with a hushed air of anticipation. The marriage of a billionaire's heiress daughter to a movie star heartthrob was a big event.

"What do you get out of this?" the groom whispered against her cheek as a pop star started to sing the first vocal.

Ellie shivered in reaction to his nearness. Glancing up through several layers of veil that helped her resemble the heiress, she murmured. "The dress. You?"

"Land."

Ellie gazed at the vocalist, but her brain swirled. The groom's warm breath on her cheek sent an exciting tingle along her nerves . . . and changed her outlook in an instant.

The wedding consultant had planned every detail of this ceremony for the heiress. Except now, Ellie appeared in all this extravagance as the substitute bride.

Arriving in New York two weeks earlier, she had never dreamed of being part of anything this grand. Pretending to be the bride made Ellie wish she could keep this groom for real.

One glance at his crooked grin turned her insides to putty. It didn't hurt that he stood head and shoulders over the other men in the wedding party, or that his wide shoulders gave the impression of strength. He looked like a dream.

Actually, he looked like Shawn Thorpe, the movie star groom. It wasn't just the way he looked. Something more than his appearance was affecting Ellie. Standing near him pulled at emotions she hadn't experienced before.

She risked another glance at him. Dark eyes filled with humor glinted back at her from a face she was sure she'd seen in movies. Or had she? With his striking resemblance to the movie star, he must be a relative, which explained his participation in this fake wedding.

Maybe they couldn't find a look-alike. Was this really the movie star?

"Are you him?" Ellie murmured just as the song ended.

The minister's voice droned over her fluttering nerves. This was the trickiest part of the charade. One slip would ruin the staged wedding. Her future depended on pulling this wedding off without a hitch. She prayed the other actors in this ceremony were as desperate to succeed as she was.

If she and the groom convinced the guests they were watching media sweethearts Shawn and Dawn get married, she would earn her ticket to success. And all thanks to the bride's father. The reclusive billionaire had staged this charade to protect his daughter from unwanted media attention.

Ellie's reward for substituting for the bride was the designer wedding gown she wore.

Studying the Sae Wong original would help her learn how to make a name for herself as a seamstress.

Asheboro wasn't New York City, but she wanted to be the best seamstress in her hometown. More than anything, Ellie wanted to make her name count.

The groom touched her hand. She trembled. She felt fragile beside him. At five foot eight, she wasn't—but she could pretend for a few minutes, couldn't she?

Ellie took pride in her ability to take care of herself. Still, a thrill raced through her as the groom gazed down into her eyes. *It's an act*, she repeated silently as her stomach fluttered. The expression in his smoldering brown eyes made her knees weak.

This groom might not be a movie star, but he could act. He knew that a real groom looked at his bride with his heart in his eyes. Ellie absorbed that look, knowing that her secret wish was to belong to someone who loved her that much.

She smothered a gasp in response to his look of devotion. Her knees going weak from his touch, she wanted to follow her pretend groom into the sunset.

That thought almost made her giggle out loud. Okay, so her heart didn't know the difference between real heated glances and talented acting, but her brain did, right?

The groom squeezed her hand, drawing her attention back to the ceremony. "No, I'm not him," he whispered against her cheek in a move that would look as if he had kissed her.

Ellie's heart skipped. He might not be the real groom, but he took her breath away. Not good! She needed to focus.

The minister's voice rose. "Repeat after me, please. I . . ."

A rumbling cough from the direction of the organ caught Ellie off guard. The loud noise smothered the minister's words.

". . . take thee . . ."

Ellie didn't hear the groom's name because of another loud cough, from a different direction this time. Everything was fine so far. Now, if she could just pull off the loving bride role. Taking a deep breath, she turned a loving gaze toward the groom. This was her chance. All she had to do was practice her acting skills.

It wasn't difficult. It didn't feel like acting. She could stare into his melting gaze for hours. But that wasn't part of her plan.

Forcing her attention back to the ceremony, Ellie

mumbled her response in a breathy whisper that wasn't acting at all.

"And now the groom . . ."

Ellie was so intent on looking at the groom and listening to the sound of his deep voice that she forgot to expect an interruption.

A loud sneeze sounded over the minister's words.

Ellie suspected that the guests were ready to strangle the people who had managed to obliterate the most important part of the ceremony. But so far, the identities of the substitute bride and groom were secure.

"I now pronounce you husband and wife. You may kiss the bride."

Kiss the bride!

Oh no! Her blood hummed. This ceremony needed to look real, but Ellie wasn't sure she would survive a kiss from this groom.

A thought occurred to her as she reeled at the possibility of being held in his arms. With all the careful planning to make the wedding look real, no one had thought of the danger of the wedding kiss.

With her hair piled on top of her head and multiple layers of veil covering her face, she could pass for the famous heiress.

Unless the groom uncovered her face!

"Don't lift the veil," Ellie hissed as the groom leaned near.

His eyes, like deep pools of chocolate, laughed at her, and then his glance dropped to her lips.

Ellie shuddered and fought the urge to lick her lips in anticipation.

He intended to kiss her. The wicked glint in his eyes dared her to try to stop the ritual. She should stop him, even at the risk of blowing her cover.

Something inside her warned that one kiss from this man would change everything. But good sense deserted her. In that instant, she wanted his kiss with every fiber of her being.

"Don't—"

His mouth absorbed her whisper as he eased the tulle up just enough to give him room to brush his warm velvety lips against hers. Then his lips settled on hers for a kiss that rocked her very soul. Heat ricocheted through her.

This wasn't her first kiss. But the burst of emotion racing along her veins would stay in her mind forever.

She heard a sigh. She wasn't sure if the sound came from the guests or from herself. One thing she knew for sure: this groom knew how to kiss.

Her brain begged for more as he dropped the veil. It was a good thing they had an audience so she couldn't beg him to kiss her again.

The maid of honor nudged Ellie with the bridal bouquet as organ music filled the church. She clutched the handful of flowers and forced a wide smile as they turned to face the guests.

A sea of faces danced before her. Nervous giggles threatened as she realized she had never seen so many hats in her entire life. The groom tucked her hand under his arm in a romantic gesture right out of the old movies she loved. The vocalist began the final song. Ellie's heart raced in time with her brain. The groom pulled her close to his side. She felt as treasured as if she were a real bride.

Suddenly, it all seemed too much. Her lips felt stiff from smiling. She concentrated on her goal and glued her gaze to the groom's face, but reality returned.

Tremors ripped through her. Her lips twitched. If she kept up this goofy look for much longer, her face would freeze in this adoring expression. A wave of giggles shook her.

"Don't you dare laugh!" he murmured through a grin.

Ellie glimpsed a twinkle in his eyes and clamped her lips shut. If she had to have a stand-in groom, she would vote for this man any day. As she stared at his good-looking face, with its slightly crooked nose and firm jaw, she realized he looked like a dream.

Too bad this wedding wasn't real.

As the vocalist sang about true love, Ellie swished the skirts of the wedding gown in an effort to get her mind back in focus. The sound of priceless fabrics whispering around her legs reminded her of what she had to do. She needed to ignore her growing attraction to this man and focus on acting the happy bride. Soon this gown would belong to her!

The music changed. Ellie took a deep breath. A dramatic note sounded. Her smile widened. The groom pressed her hand close to his side, and she felt the heat and power radiating from his body. Reactions tingled along her arm. She forced herself to concentrate. This was it. All that kept her from owning an exclusive Sae Wong wedding gown was this march down the aisle.

And suddenly, after a whirlwind dash, they were at the back of the church. The wedding director, wearing a phone headset, snapped orders into the mike as she motioned Ellie and the groom toward a door behind her.

Sae Wong's assistant appeared in the opening and pulled Ellie through the door, snapping it shut behind the groom. "Hurry, this way, before someone notices."

"Won't people ask where we are?" Ellie gasped, as she tried to keep pace with the assistant's fast lope down the long hall. But the gown twisted around her legs and yards of veil floated from side to side, pulling on her hair. The groom's grip on her arm kept her moving.

The assistant shoved open a door. "No," she said as she turned to wave at a uniformed chauffeur standing at the end of the long hallway. "The bride's white limo will pull around in front of the church as the guests are coming out. Everyone will think they've seen the wedding couple pass by." She pointed across the hall and nodded to the groom. "Change in there. Hurry!"

"I didn't bring clothes." Ellie turned to the assistant who had guided her studies at the designer's studio for the past two weeks. "I put this gown on before the limo picked me up at the hotel."

"I brought your things." The assistant nodded to Ellie's case on the floor by a child-sized chair. "It's a good thing we had you stay in the hotel last night. Otherwise, I wouldn't have been able to get your clothes."

Ten minutes later, Ellie shoved her feet into white Reeboks as a knock sounded on the door.

"He's ready. Are you?" The assistant zipped the long garment bag. "Everything's in here: the veil, the gown.

Here, put the heels in your case." She shoved the matching sandals at Ellie. "You saved our skin, Ellie. We couldn't have pulled this off without your help."

"It was fun, but—"

The knock sounded again.

"Come on, you have to hurry." The assistant twirled for one last check of the room. "Take your hair down as soon as you get in the car. You don't favor the bride as much with your hair loose." She opened the door, then turned back. "What were you going to ask?"

"Will Shawn and Dawn get married today?"

The assistant checked her watch and smiled as she motioned Ellie through the door. "By the time you are packed and ready to leave town, the deed will be done." She glanced at the groom waiting outside the door. "Remember, don't breathe a word of this to anyone."

"Okay!" The groom turned to Ellie. "You're leaving with me, right?"

"I . . ."

"Yes!" The assistant turned to Ellie. "It's best if he drops you off."

"I was planning to take the bus."

"No! We can't risk anyone spotting you and putting things together." The assistant pushed Ellie toward the groom. "We've managed to pull this off so far. Don't let us down now: ride with him." The assistant nodded toward the six-foot-four bundle of male filling up the hallway. "We picked the perfect groom, Ellie. He's a great guy. Now get out of here . . . and watch the news." The note of amusement in her voice spoke volumes about her relieved tension. "Keep in touch."

Ellie heard the last words as the door almost caught the end of the garment bag she struggled to control along with her case.

"Here, let me." He swung the cumbersome bag between two fingers. Then his long denim-clad legs raced across the parking lot toward a large black truck.

Ellie laughed as she jogged behind. In that truck, they would surely stick out in New York traffic. So much for keeping out of sight. Another snicker escaped on a nervous bubble of tension.

"What?" The groom glanced over his shoulder as he stuffed the garment bag in the extended cab.

"Hey, watch out. That dress is worth a lot of money."

"Right!" He grabbed her case and pushed it under the garment bag. "So is my part of this deal." He half-lifted her into the passenger seat. "And there's no way I'll collect if anyone spots the name on that bag and guesses the truth."

From her elevated position on the high seat, Ellie absorbed the view. His tall body looked powerful. Broad shoulders filled the plaid button-up shirt he wore, leaving little room for so much as a wrinkle. His wedding tuxedo hadn't needed shoulder padding, she noticed. Where had this man come from? If he stayed in town long, some talent scout would be giving him a screen test.

The thought made her grin as she waggled her fingers in his face as he closed the door. His answering scowl brought her to giggles. She shouldn't tease. He was right. Just because she had her reward in hand gave her no right to risk his with careless actions.

"It's kind of you to give me a lift. I had planned to take the bus."

"With that bag?" He snorted as he slammed the driver's side door.

"Okay, it's not far. If you'll just drop me off, I'd appreciate it." No sense in needling him. He looked ready to burst a seam, as it were. She didn't blame him. They had spent the past hour acting like a loving couple in front of hundreds of guests expecting to see the latest media darlings get married. This wedding had made news headlines for months.

"Where are you staying?"

"Two blocks down from Fifth Avenue." Ellie reached to fasten her seat belt as the engine roared to life. "Do you know your way around the city?"

"Sorta," he said as he glanced to be sure the street was clear before pulling out of the parking lot. Once they turned into the side street, it was easy to see the traffic congestion all around the massive church. "Good thing I asked about alternate routes before the ceremony." He turned left, just missing the traffic jam. "Give me directions when we get close."

"I really appreciate this . . ." Her words trailed off as she twisted toward him. "I don't even know your name!"

"Samuel Clay Oglethorpe." He held out a large hand that felt rough in hers. "Sam to my friends."

"Emiline Anastasia Gray, Ellie to my husbands." Ellie laughed, but her insides quivered as heat from his touch raced up her arm. What was happening here? His responding chuckle eased her tension. But he had let go of her hand.

"Do you have many husbands?"

"You wore contacts," she blurted as she noticed the teasing green glint in the hazel eyes watching her. "Oh, that reminds me." She pulled pins out of her hair until it fell to her shoulders. "That feels better. Your eyes aren't as dark as Shawn's."

Sam glanced in her direction, noticing the way the light glistened in her sandy-colored locks. "Your hair isn't as dark as Dawn's. How did they expect to keep the guests from noticing the difference?"

Ellie leaned over her lap. "No one saw me without the veil. With all the hair gook, my natural color was dark enough." She settled back in the seat and grinned.

"So you wore contacts too!"

"I didn't have a choice."

"Green eyes would be a dead giveaway. Dawn's eyes are dark brown." He glanced away from the street. "The difference in your appearance is amazing!"

"You mean you don't see an heiress when you look at the real me?" Ellie teased as he wove the vehicle through traffic. With every fiber of control she had learned over the years, she tried to ignore the tension that twisted her insides.

Why did it matter what this man thought? Her attraction to him made no sense. There wasn't room in her life for a man. With his looks and charm, a man like Sam spelled trouble. A girl couldn't keep her mind on her work with him around.

Still, she wondered what he saw when he looked at

her as Ellie, not as the bride. "Oh, slow down. I recognize that tall building . . ."

Sam motioned toward all the skyscrapers along the street and grunted.

Ellie's tension escaped on a giggle as she read his expression. "Okay, I know, all the buildings in New York are tall. The red one, well, the darkest one that's red, beside the gray . . . there in the next block. Do you see it?"

Sam's laugh came from deep in his chest and filled the truck. Ellie tilted her chin in pretended offense. But with humor illuminating his face, Sam was so handsome he took her breath away, and she couldn't hold a straight face. She rolled her eyes and laughed.

"It's a good thing you aren't driving. Where are you from, anyway?"

"North Carolina," Ellie said as she tossed her hair back, staring at the numerous lanes of traffic. "I don't think it's odd that I don't know my way around a strange city. . . . Oops, that's the turn."

It was a good thing Sam's driving was better than her directions. Horns tooted, brakes squealed, but he made the turn as Ellie watched her building entrance appear. "There, two buildings up on the right."

"You're staying at the Y?" The incredulous note in his voice revealed his reaction to the rundown building that was all Ellie could afford.

Okay, so she had played the part of the bride in a big society wedding. That wasn't her world. Far from it, in fact.

"Thank you for the lift." Her tone would have left frost on a pumpkin, but she wasn't about to explain her situation.

In her book, good manners and a sense of humor went a long way. Sam had both, and good looks to boot. . . . Well, his manners had been good, until that last comment.

She unbuckled the seatbelt with a loud snap. "Thanks, I can manage from here."

"Whoa . . . what's the rush? How long are you staying in town?" Sam's glance held her frozen in place. "I'm from North Carolina too. Maybe we could go get some dinner and talk about home?"

"Oh!" Her heart leaped to her throat. Despite his reaction to her lodging, she liked him. He had made the stress of the role-playing easier. But the wedding was over. This feeling digging into her ribs was probably tension. She couldn't feel attached to a man she had known for a couple of hours, even if she had married him.

Besides, there was no use dragging this out. She hated goodbyes. Always had, always would. That's how her life had started—with a goodbye she couldn't even remember.

"It's been fun, Sam, but I have to go." A great exit line. Too bad she had to turn back when she couldn't move the seat. "Um, would you help me get this bag out?"

"How about dinner? I don't know about you, but now that the show's over, I'm hungry enough to eat the legs off a chair."

Ellie's good humor returned as she heard the phrase.

"I know. I skipped breakfast." Her gaze roamed over his face one last time. "I have to pack. I'm taking the bus home tonight."

Sam frowned. "You're planning to lug that bag all the way home on a bus?"

His tone made her feel about two feet tall. Okay, so she wished she didn't have to ride the bus. But driving in New York City took experience.

"Okay," Ellie said as she moved to reach past the wall that was his chest as he stopped by her side. A quick glance found his eyes boring into her. Shrugging, her right hand fisted on her hip, she sighed. "It seemed to be the best choice considering I haven't been to New York before."

"Hey! Why don't you ride home with me?" Sam glanced at the passing traffic. "I'm headed back tonight too." He watched doubt race across her expressive face. "It would beat fighting that garment bag on a bus for two days."

"Are you really from North Carolina?"

"Sure," Sam said as he pointed to the back of his truck. "Look at the license plate."

The *First in Flight* emblem blared at her in red, white, and blue letters from the truck's bumper. Honking beeps of harassed drivers filled the air. For a few seconds, she felt a connection to home just by looking at the metal tag on his vehicle. How could she be homesick? She didn't have a home to go back to. "Where?"

"Redbud, near Pilot Mountain. What about you?"

"Asheboro."

He nodded. "The State Zoo, right?" Horns blasted near the truck's bumper. Sam's lips spread in a crooked grin she couldn't resist. "Go get your bags. We can talk on the way home without breathing these exhaust fumes." His grin spread across very kissable lips.

She should know. His kiss at the wedding had warmed her to the core. Shaking her head to clear away thoughts of how right it had felt to be in his arms, she said, "I—"

"Grab your stuff. Let's get out of town before traffic picks up."

"But—"

"It makes no sense to take a bus when you have a comfortable ride waiting to drop you at your door." Sam felt the muscles in his jaw tighten. It made no sense that he was offering to chauffeur this girl home, either. What had happened to his brain? Ellie Gray wasn't his business. Just because they'd been partners in a fake wedding ceremony didn't mean he needed to take care of her now.

Why did he care how she got home? Was it because her green eyes seemed too large in a face framed by sandy-blond hair?

He didn't have time to be attracted to a female. He needed to focus on his goal of reclaiming his family's property. Once he accomplished that, he could think about his future.

After Shawn's joking around at the bachelor party, he wouldn't rest easy until he had the deed to his property signed and notarized.

He didn't trust his cousin's sense of humor. It would

never do for Ellie to learn about the challenge Shawn had thrown in his face last night.

He and Shawn were the only two people at the party who had known Sam would be standing at the altar the next day. Shawn's inexhaustible sense of humor taunted Sam with the offer of free land. All he had to do—

"I—"

A nearby horn blared so loud Sam couldn't hear her words. "Look, traffic is getting worse." He waved an impatient hand toward the mass of vehicles lining the street. "Do you want a ride or not?"

Chapter Two

"Why the guilty look?" Sam snapped his cell phone shut as Ellie hurried toward the truck. He had spent the last few minutes rearranging his life, a conflict of action that he wanted to deny even to himself. He pretended he didn't know why he was doing this, but in his gut, he knew. If he didn't admit he was attracted to Ellie, maybe this new headache would go away.

He glanced at his watch.

"You still have a couple of minutes to spare." He stepped forward and reached for her bags. "I've never met a woman I didn't have to wait on. This is great."

"Like men are always on time," Ellie scoffed as she stood on tiptoe to climb into the cab. "I'm ready when you are."

"I called the hotel. I'll pack and get checked out in about thirty minutes." Sam started the engine and glanced over to see the look of amusement on her face. "What?" He could get used to those sparkling green eyes and that grin.

"Nothing," Ellie said as she twirled a strand of hair around her finger and shrugged. "I was just thinking . . . that's triple the time I needed."

"Okay, you win." Sam frowned at the rush of cars in front of him and tried to control a shudder. Something about his last words scared him. She had won all right. But the question was what? Had the glow of humor from her luminous eyes worked a spell on him?

His reaction to her had nothing to do with her figure. No way! He kept his gaze above her shoulders the whole time. A man could take only so much—and one glance at Ellie in faded jeans and a form-fitting white blouse had been his limit. She was like a long cold drink of water: unassuming, but oh, so satisfying.

He hadn't been able to get her out of his mind from the moment she started down the aisle.

That's why he had offered her a lift home. He had planned to stay in New York for a few days. What was he thinking? A honking horn jolted him to attention. New York City traffic was bad enough without him fantasizing about the substitute bride.

May as well enjoy it while it lasts, chump. If she ever finds out about that dare, it will be all over. What? What would be all over? What was he thinking? He didn't need any emotional upheaval in his life. And he didn't need a woman like Ellie Gray. She was spunky, determined, and as cute as a pug-nosed pup, but she wasn't what he needed in his life. So why had he offered her a ride home?

Sam clamped his teeth together so hard his jaw ached as he recalled Shawn's challenge. He should have known. From the minute he answered the phone and Shawn said, "Hey, buddy," he should have expected something to go wrong.

How many times in the past had he fallen in with a scheme of Shawn's?

Sam forced his mind off the past and glanced at Ellie. "Are you hungry? We can eat at the hotel, or wait for a fast-food joint along the way."

"Let's wait. I have some crackers in my bag."

Sam opened his mouth, then changed his mind. Did she think he expected her to pay for a meal at his hotel? He had noticed she had stayed in the cheapest accommodations in the city. He started to explain, but a glance in her direction caused the words to freeze in his throat.

With her shoulders back and her chin tilted high, Ellie Gray had pride written all over her. Who was this girl? How had she let herself get talked into this pretend wedding in the first place?

"Okay. I'll grab a couple of drinks from the machine on the way out. What do you like?"

"I haven't had a Pepsi since I got to New York."

With her bottle-green eyes glowing like spotlights, Sam found it difficult to concentrate on parking the truck. "Do you want to wait in the lobby?"

Ellie glanced over her shoulder at the garment bag

with Sae Wong's name spelled out in glittering letters. "I'll stay here."

Sam frowned. The area looked safe enough in daylight. "Are you sure?"

"Don't worry about me."

"This isn't Asheboro, you know."

"Will you go on, already?" She nodded toward the backseat. "You don't think anybody's going to get me out of this truck without my dress, do you?"

"I'll hurry." *Independent women are a pain*, Sam thought as he entered the elegant lobby and strode toward the checkout desk.

Five minutes later, the room service order placed, he dashed for the elevators. He didn't want to take thirty minutes to check out. A grin relaxed the muscles of his face as he considered the ribbing he would get if he were late. Her sense of humor was one of the things he liked about Ellie.

In less than twenty minutes he tossed two weeks' worth of clothing into his bags, signed the tab, and dashed back to the truck, his hands filled with luggage and the bag from room service. "Open the door!" he growled.

"Sorry," she said, her eyes sparkling at his scowl. "You took so long I thought I'd take a nap." Ellie opened his door and slipped back to her seat. "Hey, you haven't used all your time yet." She winked and showed him the time. "You still have a minute to go."

Sam felt a laugh start low in his chest as tension left his body. Ellie did that to him, made him want to laugh.

It felt good to roll his eyes and pretend to be impatient. He remembered this same lighthearted feeling from the past. Was he flirting with Ellie? "So, now you know. I'm a man of my word."

Ellie allowed an unladylike snort to escape. When Sam laughed, her insides melted. She had to get a life. Having the determination to stick to her work was great, but long hours of effort had left her feeling vulnerable. "Then let's get going."

Had she made a mistake? Accepting a ride with Sam was risky, even if it saved her pocketbook. Every minute she spent with him made her want the things she couldn't afford, things like a husband . . . and a family.

Usually, she felt more at ease when she treated a man like a friend. But Sam made her feel different. Thrills raced through her as she remembered her first glimpse of him standing at the front of the church, waiting for the pretend bride. He had looked so handsome he had taken her breath away. Was it any wonder she'd jumped at the chance to spend more time with him?

She frowned. She was closed up in this vehicle with a man who fit her daydreams to perfection, and she couldn't do a thing about it.

What choice did she have? She didn't have a job, a home, or a name. She was stuck. Until she got this sewing business started, she had nothing to offer. A man like Sam, a man who would travel hundreds of miles to help family, deserved a woman of substance.

Ellie wasn't sure how she knew anything about the man at her side. It was just a feeling, like how she knew the white Stetson he'd tossed on the dress bag suited him better than a baseball cap would have.

Sam pulled into traffic. "With luck we can get out of town before the evening rush. Pull a couple of sandwiches out of that bag." He nodded at the room service container. "Drinks are in the bottom."

"You got food?"

"Room service!"

"Can you eat while you drive in this traffic?"

"Honey, in this traffic I'll have time to eat at the stoplights."

Ellie unwrapped the club sandwich, thick with shaved slices of turkey and ham, and passed it over, while her mind wrapped around the word he had used. She wasn't sure how she felt about him calling her *honey*.

Two stoplights later, the sandwiches were gone. Ellie put the wrappers and drink cans in the bag, which still felt full. "What have you got packed in here?"

"Comfort food." Sam grinned as he negotiated the stream of traffic. He had noticed the worn case she carried. If he guessed right, she had spent very little on food during her stay in town. Besides, driving gave him an appetite. He had ordered enough food to get them past the congested areas of their trip. "Pass me an apple, please."

Munching on a Granny Smith apple that was tart enough to strip the paint off his vehicle, Sam steered through the packed streets. As his tension eased—he'd been wound tight for that wedding fiasco—he darted glances at his passenger.

Ellie attacked her apple like a girl, nibbling little bites around the middle—nothing like the chunk he'd bitten off. While he watched, she twisted and turned, looking at everything they passed. She had said this was her first trip to New York. Sam suspected this was her first trip anywhere.

"Ellie!" He tested her name and met her startled glance. "What was the rest of your name?"

"Emiline Anastasia Gray."

"That's a mouthful." He grinned. "Your parents sure made it hard for you to learn to spell."

Ellie stared through the windshield at the passing buildings. "I was named after the two elderly ladies who found me on the church steps."

"Oh . . . sorry."

"Emiline and Anastasia," she said as she met his frowning glance with a grin. "I was wrapped in a dingy blanket so they picked Gray for my last name."

"I see." Sam's quiet words gave away none of the emotional whirlwind going on in his gut. He felt like a jackass. He had stormed into New York determined to confront his cousin over a piece of property as if it were the most important thing in the world, while Ellie had gone through her whole life without even knowing her real name. That would teach him to overreact. It was time he put things in perspective. His personal life would be a good place to start.

"The old maid sisters thought I should have a distinctive name since I didn't have anything else in this world." Ellie's eyes sparkled with a suspicious glint, but a laugh gurgled past her lips. "It worked, don't you think?"

"Yeah, it worked." Sam's gut crawled with emotions he didn't want to analyze. He forced a grin in answer to her attempt at humor. What else could he do? He had stumbled into a personal area of her past, but she was letting him off easy. "That's a fine name. I like Ellie."

He welcomed the need to focus on his driving. He felt like kicking his own backside all the way across the Brooklyn Bridge. He hadn't had parents either, but he'd had his grandparents.

"So, were you born in Pilot Mountain?"

Sam gritted his teeth. Okay, he had started this conversation. He had opened his big mouth and started asking personal questions. Now he'd have to be civil, at least. "Yeah." He steered past a car pulled to the side of the narrow street. "Redbud, near enough. Do you know the area?"

"No, but from pictures I've seen it looks nice."

"Yeah!" His fingers tightened around the steering wheel. It was home—or it would be when he acquired the land from Shawn. Guilt nagged at his conscience as he thought about the careless suggestion Shawn had offered as an easy way for him to get that land. Ellie didn't deserve to be a pawn in one of Shawn's jokes.

"Do you think Shawn and Dawn are married yet?"

Sam flinched as her words appeared on the same wavelength as his thoughts. "Almost," he said as he checked his watch. "Thanks to our help." He grinned. "The attendants caught a helicopter to the airport, then a short flight on a private jet. Shawn and Dawn should be saying their vows about now."

"I hope so." Ellie turned toward him and smiled. "They went to a lot of trouble to have a private wedding."

"Yeah," Sam said as he forced his glance to the rows of cars in front of him. Ellie was amazing. Her life was far from perfect, but she worried about a wealthy couple getting their wish. "Shawn reached his limit with the media." Sam took the exit that led to the interstate, and home. "He said there were more important things going on in the world than his wedding." Sam met her gaze. "Makes you appreciate the guy."

"I'm glad we helped." Ellie cleared her throat, but he heard the hint of emotion as she continued. "You and Shawn are close?"

Sam understood the wistful note in her voice now that he knew she didn't have a family.

"He's my cousin. We grew up together." And fought like cats and dogs. But she didn't need to know that. Few people understood the rivalry between the two cousins. Shawn loved the challenge. But to Sam, their scraps had meant something.

A bitter taste filled his mouth. He regretted many things from that period in his life. Shawn was a decent guy. Losing the land hadn't been his fault, but he had egged Sam on at every turn, increasing the conflict Sam felt. Even at the bachelor party.

Shawn had finally agreed to sell the land. Still, Sam was glad he had been there to help Shawn escape from the press. It didn't hurt that he could buy back his family's property as well. "Shawn's an alright guy."

"Why did you do it, Sam?"

Her question pierced the thoughts going around his mind. He felt as if a tub of ice water had been dumped on his head. He should have expected the question. After asking about her name—not that he'd had a clue he was broaching a troublesome topic—he owed her an answer.

Sam cleared his throat and checked the rearview mirror. "I . . . I want to buy some property from Shawn."

"You went through all this for a pile of dirt?" Ellie shook her head in disbelief. "You came all the way to New York, and impersonated a famous movie star at the wedding of the century, just so you could buy some land?"

Gritting his teeth, he shoved the gas pedal to the floor, and mumbled under his breath. "Yeah," he said, but his grip on the steering wheel eased when he noticed her confused expression.

Okay, he knew his actions seemed out of proportion to the situation. But Ellie didn't know the whole story.

"Shawn's . . . a busy guy. I don't see much of him anymore." Not since he changed his name ten years ago. "When he called, I took a chance and here I am." *And what a mess I'm in now. I don't have the land. The deal isn't even in writing.* And his passenger was a stranger who made him question his motives and his sanity.

"You must be good friends for you to go to all that trouble." Ellie paused. "Shawn's from your mother's side of the family?"

"Nope," he said with a curse under his breath. Ellie

had touched a raw nerve. Leave it to a woman to dig at a sore spot. Even an innocent like this girl, with no way of knowing his family history, had found his weak spot. "Shawn dropped part of his surname for show business."

"Oh!"

Sam heard the amazement in her voice. He understood her reaction. She didn't have a name, or any clue as to her family, and Shawn had denied his family by changing his name. The old resentment pushed against Sam's control.

"So, he's from your father's side of the family."

Sam sensed more questions. For the life of him, he wasn't sure he could hold his temper much longer. He suspected her lack of family spurred her interest. But he would rather she talked about something else.

"What about you?" He met her questioning glance. "You went to a lot of trouble, and all you got was a wedding dress."

His brow arched when he saw her reaction. He had done it now. Green sparks flew from her eyes. Man, she was cute when she got riled. His muscles tightened in tension. This could get embarrassing.

"That isn't just any dress. It's a Sae Wong original!"

"So?"

"Don't you recognize the designer's name?" Ellie twisted around in the confines of the seatbelt, pulled her knee up on the seat, and leaned toward him. "Sae Wong is famous."

Sam heard the awe in her tone as he forced his attention back to the road. With her eyes spitting sparks, and her expressions changing with almost every word, she was an eyeful. Not to mention the picture she made leaning toward him, her curves filling the front of her shirt . . . and his fantasies. He needed a cold drink. "Any more Pepsi in that bag?"

"I thought everyone recognized Sae Wong's name." Ellie reached for the drinks. "Don't you read magazines?" She pulled the tab on the can and passed it over.

"Not the ones you read." Sam took a swig from the can. Her fascination with the designer was understandable. Sam suspected the woman's well-known identity appealed to Ellie. "I don't read fashion magazines." He grinned at the sound of her frustrated sigh. That'd teach her to jump to conclusions. "So, how did you get involved in all this wedding mess when you live in Asheboro?"

"I was studying at Sae Wong's studio."

"Oh!" He frowned. "Why didn't Dawn wear the dress at the real wedding?"

A gloating expression covered her face. Sam doubted she realized how cute she looked with her glittering eyes and that smile on her face.

"Dawn commissioned Sae Wong to design two wedding dresses." She rolled her eyes. "Can you believe it? Two gowns?"

"Two wedding dresses?"

Ellie grinned. She was allowed. She had shown her own amazement in front of the designer and half of Sae

Wong's assistants. She was due a little smirking of her own. "Dawn couldn't decide which one she liked."

"What's the big deal?" Sam tooted the horn at a driver trying to cut in too close. "A dress is a dress!"

"That's a typical male reaction." Ellie lifted her chin and glared.

"You looked great in the dress you wore."

"Thanks," Ellie said past the emotions that almost blocked her throat. That was the nicest compliment she had ever had.

But she couldn't let his attention go to her head. She took another gulp of her drink. When she got out of this truck, she had to get to work. She didn't have time for daydreams and fake grooms. Not if she planned to keep a roof over her head.

"Dawn's father planned to cancel the wedding?" Sam asked.

Ellie nodded. "After some photographer slipped past the security system at the family estate and gave them a fright. Sae Wong was stuck with two wedding dresses, ten attendants' gowns, and the mother of the bride's outfit."

Sam whistled. "Bet that adds up to a few bucks."

"Half a million dollars in dresses left in Sae Wong's lap." Then she had spotted Ellie in her studio. "That's why I wore one of the dresses." A wistful expression erased the humor from Ellie's features. "I could get married in that dress."

She stared out at the dark silhouettes of trees left by the late afternoon sun. She felt as if a shadow, like the ones on the road, had passed over her heart. She would

make the best of what she had, like always. And someday . . . someday she would have a real wedding.

"You wanted the dress because you're planning to
get married?" He sounded incredulous.

"I wish!" A flush of color rushed to Ellie's face. She
had thought she had outgrown the tendency to blush. "I
mean, I wish I didn't have to take the dress apart."

"What?"

Ellie grinned. His shocked exclamation sounded like
a kindred spirit, instead of a man who knew nothing
about dressmaking. "I need to study the techniques
used to make the dress."

"Are you crazy? That dress must be worth—"

"Thousands! I know," she finished in an awed whisper. "But I'll learn everything I need to know about
sewing formal dresses from that gown." Sam shook his
head as if he thought she'd lost her mind. Maybe she
had. "People do it all the time."

What choice did she have? She could learn only so
much in the two weeks she'd been in New York. This
was something she had to do. "Haven't you ever wanted something so bad you'd do anything to get it?"

Sam recognized the emotions that turned her face to
a mask. The bunched-up shoulders, the tension that he
knew tied her body in knots. He knew exactly what
Ellie was talking about. From the sound of it, they were
two of a kind. Two people twisted by what life had
thrown their way. Two people who wanted things to be
different so bad they could taste it. Yeah, he knew what
she meant.

He could remember when he first heard the story of

the Oglethorpe property, of his lost heritage. From that day on, he had never forgotten that his grandfather had gambled away the family land.

The worst part was that his grandfather had lost the land to his own brother, Shawn's grandfather—who had made sure his grandfather never forgot his loss. But—and this was the kicker, the thing that stuck in Sam's craw like a burr under a saddle—his grandfather had continued to work the land he'd lost. The gall of it made Sam see red. How could his great-uncle have squashed the pride of his own brother?

Sam forced his attention to the highway. But his insides twisted. That was what had driven him . . . all through high school, college, and now, years later, to New York City. Oh, yeah, he knew what it was like to want something so bad you'd do anything to get it.

He had pretended to be his famous cousin in a wedding ceremony, hadn't he? He had swallowed his pride and responded to Shawn's call for help. What choice did he have?

Shawn had been both his friend and his opponent. Sam had studied to pursue his love of the environment. Shawn had pursued his interest in an acting career. Both had achieved success. But through it all, Shawn held on to the one thing Sam wanted most, his land.

Even when Shawn changed his name, which in Sam's opinion was like disowning family, he had retained ownership of that land. Shawn had inherited the Oglethorpe coastal estate, where he lived. It was his favorite property. Sam preferred the mountain property. The mountain behind his house was in his blood. He felt like part of the mound of earth and stone. Pilot Mountain was home.

Yet Shawn controlled the family land in the foothills of the Blue Ridge Mountains. Sam knew his cousin hadn't set foot on the property in over ten years. But still Shawn refused to sell.

The situation caused Sam many sleepless nights. After the injustice of his grandfather's circumstances had come the worry. Why did Shawn hold on to property he never visited? What if he decided to sell?

Sam worked day and night to be in a position to buy the land his grandfather had gambled away. Then, when he'd all but given up hope of regaining his heritage, Shawn had called.

His jaw ached from gritting his teeth. Shawn had jerked his string and he had jumped. But what else could he do? He loved the family homeplace. That land was in his blood. He worked from morning until night with his tree service company to make money for the purchase.

So when Shawn called, Sam had dropped everything and made the trip to New York. He enjoyed watching Shawn twist under the same pressure he had felt when he tried to buy the property. But the fun hadn't lasted.

Despite the hard feelings between their parents and grandparents, he and Shawn had remained friends. When Shawn had asked for a favor, Sam knew he would have agreed, even if his cousin hadn't offered to sell the land.

But at the bachelor party, Shawn had thrown out a challenge, a chance for Sam to get the land free.

Chapter Three

Do you know what it's like to want something so bad you'd do anything to get it?

Ellie's words whirled around in his head as the tires circled on the road. Oh yeah, he knew what that feeling was like. That one sentence summed up his life from the year he turned ten.

He glanced across the dark cab toward Ellie's nodding form. He could barely see her in the flickering lights of oncoming cars.

He didn't need light to know what she looked like. Her image was etched on his brain: eyes the color of emeralds and sandy hair that glistened in the sun. But it was her grin, wide as a mile and warm as fudge, that played havoc with his plans.

Her eyes sparkled when she laughed, and Sam soaked up the sound of her joy. He was in tune with her in a way he had never experienced. But he couldn't show his feelings. Yet even with the warning flashing in his head, he couldn't erase her glowing face from his memory.

Was she planning to get married? His gut twisted at the thought, which made no sense. What did it matter to him?

Why couldn't he get her out of his mind? That's what scared the pants off him. Repeatedly her question spun through his mind. *Do you know what it's like to want something so bad you'd do anything to get it?* All through the rest stop in Trenton, where they had eaten the last of the hotel sandwiches, her words had taunted him.

Now, hours later, those words were spinning around his head like a broken record. And he knew why.

With his goal within reach, his fickle heart had taken a detour.

For twenty years, he had chased a dream. He had fantasized about clearing his family's name. He had dreamed, worked, and schemed. Now all he could think about was the woman by his side.

Ellie moaned in her sleep. The soft noise jerked his attention from the road for several seconds before he forced his eyes back to the winding ribbon of asphalt. Why had this happened now? With his goal in sight, why had his foolish heart changed directions?

It wasn't like him to lose focus. He listened to the whisper of Ellie's breathing as he stared into the lights of the oncoming traffic. His eyes blurred in the glare. Driving had become a chore. He reached over to shake her awake.

Ellie yawned and stretched her arms. "Are we home?"

Sam laughed for the first time in hours. Ellie had fallen asleep after leaving Trenton, but one question from her and he felt revived enough to laugh. "Almost. Are you awake?"

"Mmmmm." Another yawn escaped. "Where are we?"

"Somewhere in Pennsylvania, I think."

"Don't you know?" Her eyes snapped open. She glanced out the dark window. Unease crept over her, forcing the sleep haze away. "What do you mean?"

"I can't keep my eyes open." Sam hunched his shoulders to ease the stiffness from long hours of driving. "I keep forgetting to look at the road signs."

"That doesn't sound good." Ellie cast a doubtful glance in his direction. It had been silly of her to drop off to sleep. She should have stayed awake and talked to him to help him stay alert. "Would you like me to drive for a while?"

"I want to stop. I need a few hours' sleep. Then I'll be good as new."

"Oh." Ellie glanced out the window. Everything was dark, except for the pool of light around approaching vehicles. This didn't look like the best place to take a break, but she'd had a nap; she could keep watch.

"This exit sign says 'lodging.' Is this okay with you?" Sam barely glanced her way.

"Uh huh." No reason she should object. One exit was as good as the next when you were this far from home. Ellie tried not to think of her dwindling cash supply. She hadn't counted on spending the night in a motel.

But she had saved the money for a bus ticket. Maybe she had enough, if it was a small motel.

Sam wheeled into a Holiday Inn parking lot. "This looks good." He stopped in front of the main lobby. "You coming in?"

"I'll wait here."

"Okay." Sam slid out of the truck. The minute his feet touched pavement, his muscles let out a sigh of relief. He stretched his arms over his head with a loud groan. He hadn't realized how tense he had been over the past few hours. "Back in a minute."

Ten minutes later, he climbed back in the truck and started the engine. A quick glance at Ellie's tilted chin kept him quiet. She hadn't moved a muscle. Her back was as rigid as the radio antenna of his truck. Okay, so this might not be the best solution. But it wasn't safe for him to drive when he had to blink every five seconds to clear his vision. Even if she was uneasy, she would have to make do, that's all he knew.

Sam pulled to a stop in front of room 821. "This is it." He reached behind him to pull out his bag. "They only had the one room, a double with two full beds. Sorry, but we'll have to share."

"I'm staying in the truck."

"You can't be serious?" Sam twisted around to face her as soon as his feet hit the ground. He grabbed the door to keep it open and glared at her through the shadows cast by the hotel lights.

He had managed to keep her from paying for a room, and now she wanted to sleep in the truck.

"You'll be stiff as a board by morning." A light

breeze lifted his hair. "It gets cool at night, even in August."

Ellie shook her head without looking at him.

Sam sighed. Getting to know Ellie Gray was as tough as pulling the layers back on an onion. One minute she was all smiles and sunny disposition, and then she would withdraw. Sam rubbed a tired hand down his face to push fatigue away. It was no use—he was exhausted.

For about five seconds, his eyes fastened on the firm straight line of her lips. His third-grade teacher had twisted her lips like that when she got mad. He knew from experience, there was no reasoning with that look. With an impatient sigh, he reached for the garment bag. "Come on, I'll take the dress. Bring your bags."

Turning toward the motel door, he heard the truck door close. But when he stopped to slip the key card in the door, he felt the heat of her body against his back.

Right. He had learned a new trick. If he wanted Ellie to cooperate, all he had to do was get control of this wedding gown. Beat all he'd ever seen. She would sleep in a cold truck just to keep that dress in sight. "Look, big double beds."

Okay, there were two beds, but they were side by side in the room. Ellie swallowed to keep her heart from jumping out of her chest. What was worse, sleeping in a truck seat in the middle of a parking lot, or sleeping in a room with a man in the next bed?

She had never spent the night in the same room with a man before. Wait a second . . . the old maids had never had company. Ellie swallowed a fresh wave of panic. She had never spent the night with a man in the same *building* before. No wonder her stomach felt sick.

Well, it was time for her to grow up. She was a big girl now, in charge of her own life, her own decisions. This wasn't the worst that could happen. Sam was a kind, caring person. Yes, she was thinking more about him than she had any reason to, but he didn't know that. This was her problem. A breeze, damp and cooled by darkness, blew in the door she still held open. Ellie shivered, chilled despite the day's warm temperatures. At least she would be warm and—

"I'll take the shower first and get out of your way." Sam dropped his bags on one of the beds without looking at her.

Sam wasn't making a big deal out of sharing a room. Then she wouldn't either. After all, she could be scrunched up in a bus seat, trying to sleep with one eye open to protect her belongings.

She could do this. She was an independent woman about to start a business. "A shower sounds good." Much better than her other option, two days on a bus. "Which bed do you want?" Color rushed up her neck, heating her face. She couldn't believe she sounded so casual, like she did this every few days, and had no worries.

She was worried plenty. This was nothing like she had expected her first night with a man to be.

"Left one's fine." Sam waved toward the closets. "Does it matter?"

"No."

"I ordered pizza delivery while I was in the office."

He tossed a twenty-dollar bill on the bed. "In case they come while I'm in the shower."

Ellie stared from the money to the departing figure of the man with whom she shared a fake marriage. Sam's kind heart stuck out a mile. She knew it from all he had done since they'd met. But she wouldn't let him pay her way. She stuffed his money in the clean shirt he had left on the bed and opened her purse.

Ellie stepped out of the shower wrapped in the thin motel towel. A loud knock echoed from the bathroom door. She froze, one foot still in the tub. Her heart raced. Had she locked the door? Feeling as if the breath had been knocked out of her, Ellie stared at the knob, waiting . . .

Sam's voice came through the roar in her head. "Pizza's here. Come eat while it's hot."

Relief washed over her. What had she expected, that he'd break the door down to see her in the bath? She crammed the towel in her mouth with both fists as a fit of hysterical giggles shook her. She had a lot to learn about getting along with men.

Five minutes later, with her T-shirt sticking to her damp skin and her head wrapped in a towel, she stalked across the room in clean jeans that hid her shaking knees. Her bare feet scraped on the rough carpet. She would keep her mind on food. Besides, she was safe with Sam.

Ellie picked up a slice of pizza and a Pepsi and flopped on the empty bed before her knees dumped her on the floor. "I'm starved."

"Yeah, me too." Sam used the remote to flip through

channels on the television. "Traveling makes me hungry." He kept his eyes glued to the screen. "Why did you stuff that money in my shirt pocket?"

"I thought you were planning to drive straight through." Ellie ignored his question and kept her eyes on the pepperoni slice she was pulling off the steaming pizza.

"Too tired." A quick glance alerted him to her tilted chin. *Okay, better drop the subject of the money.* He got up to get another slice of pizza.

A peep in her direction was all he allowed himself. From the moment she'd opened the bathroom door, steam filled with her fruity scent had wrapped around his senses like a blanket of fog and started blood raging through his body.

When she appeared, wearing a clingy T-shirt and a pair of black jeans, he almost choked on the pizza in his mouth. Why did she tie him in knots? Sam turned back to the bed, all the while keeping his eyes away from where Ellie sat on the other bed.

He'd dated plenty of girls, been serious about a few, almost proposed to a couple. But none of the females in his past had caused his heart to race like this girl did. He cast a suspicious glance in Ellie's direction, then nearly choked again.

She leaned back against the head of the bed with her eyes closed. A big smile covered her face as she chewed. She looked like a cat that had finished a bowl of cream.

"I hope you like pepperoni," he croaked, almost as if he dared her to complain. What was wrong with him?

"It's perfect," she said as she turned toward him with that smile on her face.

Sam crammed half a slice of pizza in his mouth in time to smother the string of curse words that threatened. How could a female look that good with her head wrapped in a bath towel?

"You are a nice man, Sam Oglethorpe."

Sam jumped up to grab another slice of his new favorite food. He didn't feel very nice. He felt like a dirty old man.

"How old are you, anyway?"

"Twenty-six," she said. Her brow wrinkled as she glanced at him with green eyes made brighter by the whiteness of the towel around her head. "Why? How old are you?"

"Thirty-two . . . I was just wondering." He slouched back on the bed and pulled the tab on another can of Pepsi. "A man can't be too careful."

A suspicious-sounding gurgle caused his forehead to wrinkle. His face felt hot. Dang, this female would have him hog-tied by morning. "What's so funny?"

"You are so sweet, Sam." A fit of giggles escaped. "You know I'm well past legal age, but it's nice of you to imply I'm young." Her smile stretched wide. "Women love to hear they look young."

"Anything you want to watch?" Sam didn't dare respond to her compliment. "I'm about ready to turn in." His yawn was real. "How about you?"

"I guess it was the nap in the truck. I feel wide awake." She brought the pizza box over to him. "Have some more, there's no sense in wasting it."

Sam risked a quick glance. Her wide eyes and gentle smile were innocent. He reached for a slice of pizza. "How did you wangle that wedding dress out of that designer?"

Ellie winked at him. A big smile covered her face. Lifting the last piece of pizza out of the box, she settled back against the pillows. "I had something they needed real bad!"

She had his attention now. "What?"

"I looked enough like a billionaire client's daughter to pass as her double." Ellie licked her fingers.

"Why were you in New York, anyway?"

"I saw a contest for a week of wishes advertised on one of the morning news shows." She took a drink from the Pepsi can. "I wrote a letter telling why I wished I could study with a fashion designer for two weeks. I still can't believe I won!" She turned to face him. Sitting cross-legged on the bed, with her eyes sparkling like emeralds, she looked about fifteen. "It was a dream come true. The producers of the show pulled some strings and voila!" She leaned toward him. "It saved my skin, I can tell you."

Sam choked as Pepsi went down the wrong way. After a couple of coughs, with moisture pooling in his eyes, he gasped, "What do you mean?"

"Well," she said and chewed for a second, her brow wrinkled. "I want to start my own business. I want to sew for the public."

"Why?" Sam didn't know much about women's clothing, but he knew business. He suspected Ellie wouldn't make much money in something as limited as sewing.

"It's all I know how to do." Ellie shrugged, pulling the towel from her hair. Twisting her head to the side, she started to comb her fingers through the drying strands. "Miss Emiline and Miss Anastasia made sure I learned everything they knew about sewing." Ellie lifted her face and leaned toward him as she said in a low voice, "But there are a lot of details about women's clothing they didn't know."

"I'll bet."

"Anyway, I have several possible clients and lots of ideas. But I needed that special touch I couldn't learn on my own." She tossed her hair back and reached for the comb on the bed. "Then I won the contest. So there I was, in the studio and in storms this designer . . . and you know the rest."

"What now?"

"I go back home and open a shop."

"Just like that?"

Ellie rolled her eyes and laughed. "It won't be that simple." Her expression sobered. "I have to make money. But I have the shop. I'll make it work." She scrambled off the bed and headed for the bathroom. "I have to. It's my dream."

Sam's pent-up breath released in a sigh. She was a real dreamer, this kid. Did she have a clue about running a business?

"What about you?"

Sam blinked. He'd been lost in thought and hadn't

heard her come back in the room. Now she was crawling under the covers of the other bed and staring at him with big green eyes.

"What about me?"

"Well, you said you were in this for the land. You carried out your part of the bargain. Shawn will sell you the land, right?"

"Yeah, that's the plan." Sam reached over to snap off the lamp. He didn't want to talk about land. After all this time, now that Shawn had put the land within his reach, he wasn't sure it was worth the price. He darted a quick glance toward the innocent face of the substitute bride and swallowed. His cousin's dare about getting the land free hung around his neck like a block of cement. No land was worth the price Shawn offered.

Sam finally caught a few winks just before morning. He woke up with cotton in his mouth and fog in his brain. For all his good intentions, he'd managed very little sleep.

Thoughts of Ellie, a foot away on the other bed, had kept his eyes open most of the night. It had seemed so easy. Well, maybe not easy. Pulling off the fake wedding hadn't seemed like a big deal. Yet from the moment he laid eyes on Ellie, dressed in all her bridal finery, everything had changed.

He shoved the cover off and struggled to his feet. He needed a shower. And about a gallon of coffee. A soft noise from the other bed drew his reluctant gaze. Everything would be fine once he got rid of his passenger.

He slammed the bathroom door with enough force to wake the motel staff in the front office. The last thing he wanted was to have a warm, sleepy woman staring at him when he got out of the shower.

"Morning." Ellie slipped past him when he walked out of the bathroom.

Ten minutes later, she was back from a shower, looking fresh and shiny as a new morning. Sam felt like day-old pizza, all dried up around the edges and crusty. The day loomed long ahead of him. He had to get away from her and get his head back on business.

They stopped at a fast-food place for a quick breakfast. Ellie wanted to give him a big hug when he crawled into the truck with his hands full of cups and a big thermos jug of coffee. She needed caffeine. She felt tired. Her night had been one long dream—starring Sam.

He seemed different from anyone she had ever met. It wasn't just his handsome face or his powerful physique. There was so much more to Sam than good looks. She smiled at the memory of him shouldering his way out of the restaurant, his Stetson low on his forehead as he juggled the coffee container and cups. If she'd known he'd have his hands full, she would have looked for him after leaving the restroom. She expected him to be waiting in the truck.

Not Sam. He thought of everything. Ellie smiled as the aroma of hot coffee drifted past her nose. She could get used to having him around.

He made her laugh. That hadn't happened much when she lived with the elderly sisters. When he looked at her with twinkling eyes, or waggled an outrageous eyebrow, she couldn't keep from laughing. She had to stop this nonsense. There was no way she could dally after Sam. She needed to work.

While she sipped coffee and mulled over what she was afraid to wish for, the powerful truck ate up miles of interstate. She would be home soon.

"Where is this shop?"

"What?" His question startled her. "Oh, my shop?" Ellie pasted on a wide grin. It wouldn't do to let Sam guess what she'd been thinking. "It's in downtown Asheboro. The building is old, but it's perfect for a dress shop."

"Why Asheboro?"

"It's all I know. I guess I'd call it home." Ellie heard the doubt in her voice and changed the subject. "Tell me about your job." She didn't want to talk about herself. There were too many questions she didn't have answers to yet.

"I'm an arborist." He paused.

Ellie chewed on the inside of her lip for long moments while he passed cars in the slow lane. "Arborist . . ." Forcing her attention to his face, she spent several seconds admiring the man at her side. Sam was enticing enough to take her mind off her troubles, and that's what she wanted. "Sounds impressive," she said as she grinned, her good humor restored just from being with him. "Now, tell me what it means?"

Sam's brow arched as he gave her a smiling glance. "I can tell you anything you want to know about trees."

"But—"

"I operate a tree-trimming service."

"Really?" Ellie's interest caught. He cut trees to make a living? That explained the calluses on his hands and his deep tan. "Do you . . . uh . . . have much demand for that type of work?"

"It depends . . . trees die and need to be cut down. Around home ice storms cause a lot of damage." He shrugged. "I've managed to make a nest egg."

"That's great!" She sighed. "I hope I can say the same thing in a year or two."

Sam frowned. Trimming trees and whacking fabric weren't the same thing. His work was in demand. "Have you thought about going back to school? Maybe go to community college and study computers, or something?"

Another sigh whooshed by Ellie's lips as she frowned. His words touched on a worrisome topic. But it wasn't something she wanted to discuss with a stranger. How could she explain her doubts? Starting a business wasn't going to be easy. She knew that. But the fact was she didn't have any other skills that would keep a roof over her head.

"I tried school before I went to work in the pillow plant. I sewed pillows for four years before the plant shut down." She frowned. This stranger's words made her question the decisions she'd made. "I've always wanted to make clothes."

"So, get another job and sew for people on the side."

Ellie shrugged. "You paid any attention to the number of plants moving their business south of the border? Jobs around home are scarce." She sighed as she stared out the window. "I have to start over, so I may as well go for something I like."

"Why take the risk?"

Ellie stared at the flashing scenery. Interstate speed wasn't good for sightseeing. But she was thinking too hard to notice the scenery anyway. This wasn't something she'd ever told anyone before.

"When I was little, I slipped into the church during a wedding." She turned to the window. "The sisters lived next door to the church, and there were lots of weddings." Her fingers plucked at a wrinkle in her jeans. "The bride's dress was the most beautiful thing I'd ever seen. I fell in love with all the dresses." Her voice dropped to a whisper, "I felt like Cinderella. Like my fairy godmother had arrived with a special surprise, just for me."

"I'm not up on fairy tales. I thought the fairy godmother made a coach out of a pumpkin. What kind of magic was that for a little girl?"

"It was as if I'd been given a glimpse of a dream." Embarrassed color washed her face with heat. Why had she told him that? He would think she wasn't competent to be left on her own.

She realized sewing for the public was a risky venture. Not many people knew how to sew these days. Each time she got a new customer, she was amazed at how happy they were to find out about her skills. "Since that day, I've wanted to make wedding dresses. Lots of wedding dresses and prom dresses, and here I am. I have a Sae Wong wedding gown that will teach me all I need to know about making formal gowns."

* * *

Miles flew by as Sam muddled over her words. Half his brain argued that he should let it go. Ellie was a stranger. He didn't want to feel protective toward her. The other half of his brain reminded him that she was only a couple of hours away.

If she needed help, he could get to her in a hurry. Question was, why did he care? That question bothered him more than he wanted to admit.

They crossed the North Carolina state line before lunch. After a quick meal at yet another fast-food place, the afternoon sun started to shine on familiar territory. Sam asked for specific directions as he took the Asheboro exit.

"Stay on this street for a couple of blocks. Okay, pull over in front of the next building on the right."

Sam slid out of the truck with a groan of relief. It had been a long ride. He looked at the building behind Ellie, and his relief changed to concern.

A quick glance confirmed that most of the buildings in the area were uninhabited. There was traffic now, but after five o'clock, what kind of neighbors would she have? If he had this figured right, Ellie planned to live in this building. "I'll get the dress bag."

Ellie unlocked the front door. "There are hooks on the wall."

Pretending to search for a wall hanger, Sam roamed past the front room into a workroom. "I want to be sure there's no grease or anything to get on the dress." A swift glance in the back revealed a rundown half-bath and a storage room. "Looks like the front room will be the best choice." How could she live here without a kitchen?

"Thanks for the ride." Ellie resisted the urge to lock the door so he couldn't leave. Living in the shop had seemed like a good idea a month ago. But with evening approaching, she felt a flutter of unease. Or maybe she just didn't want to say goodbye to Sam.

It worried her that she'd enjoyed his company so much. It was clear she would never see him again. Why waste time dreaming?

"It was kind of you to give me a lift."

"You have my phone numbers?"

"Yes, your home phone, your cell, and your business number." She grinned, but her insides wobbled like Jell-O. No one had ever worried about her before. It gave her a warm feeling. At the same time, a chill raced down her back. It wouldn't do to start leaning on Sam.

"I'll let my friends find these numbers by accident. They'll think I have a boyfriend when they see this list." The words almost choked her. What friends? She'd lost touch with the friends she had in high school. The only people she knew these days were the few people who called to ask her to sew for them. That was another bad thing about the route she'd chosen for her life. She'd be by herself most of the time.

"When can I call to check on you?"

Hearing his concern, Ellie turned to put his numbers in her bag and blinked. Why did being around Sam make her feel helpless? It was time for him to go. She didn't want him to suspect the pickle she was in. "I'll call you as soon as I get the phone connected, okay?"

Worse than leaning on him, or having him guess her

financial situation, was the dread of saying goodbye. She managed a smile, but her lips felt numb. "It might be a day or two."

Why did saying goodbye make her feel so wretched?

Chapter Four

Sometime after dark, loud knocking on the front door of the shop had Ellie almost climbing out of her skin. She couldn't be frightened. This shop was her home. She had to get used to staying here. The noise was unexpected, that's all.

With her heart hammering in her chest, she edged along the wall, staying in the shadows. Weak illumination from the street lamp revealed a ghostly face looking in the window. Sam! Her knees sagged, almost dumping her onto the floor.

Shoving back the bolts with shaking hands, Ellie opened the door. Calling on her last thread of self-control, she managed to keep from throwing herself against his broad chest.

"This is a surprise." Did her voice quiver?

"Did I tell you I'm on vacation for the next couple of weeks?"

Warm fuzzy feelings wrapped around Ellie as she stared into his gleaming eyes. That was about all she could see in the darkness of the room. How had he managed to stay single? At thirty-two, he looked closer to her age, with that cowlick lifting his dark hair off his temple. When he grinned, he had dimples.

Or was she so relieved to see a friendly human that she would have gushed over any near-stranger?

Despite their long hours of traveling together, she knew little about Sam. What she did know would get her in trouble, fast. Heart racing, she pulled a face.

"No kidding?"

"Yeah." His grin cast an aura of charm around him like a superhero's forcefield. "I've never been to the State Zoo." He looked past her to the dark room. "I got halfway home before I realized this was the perfect opportunity."

"For what?" Ellie tried to hide her relief at seeing him, along with her sense of helplessness. She didn't want to start depending on another person. Not now. She had always stood on her own two feet. She would this time. "You lost me."

"Well . . ." he stalled. He was used to thinking fast on his feet. In his line of work, cutting down trees, trimming dead limbs, he needed a quick brain. He could get hurt if he didn't stay alert. Last winter a kid working with one of the other tree services in the area had died because of a falling limb. Oh, yeah, he needed to stay alert. So why did his tongue feel as if it were glued to the top of his mouth?

"I thought you could use an extra pair of hands getting the shop ready." Sam watched Ellie's eyes spark with temper. He knew that tilt of her chin. He'd better talk fast. "In exchange, I was hoping for a guide to the zoo."

"I've never been to the zoo, sorry." Ellie's temper flared because his suggestion tempted her. She couldn't let this happen! Hanging her hopes on Sam spelled trouble. It was safer to get rid of him now. Gaining strength from her new resolve, she pushed on the door. "Have fun."

Sam kept the door open with one hand as he watched expressions chase across Ellie's face. He had a bad feeling about this whole thing. He'd bet his best chainsaw she was glad to see him.

"Hey, wait!" He felt her pushing against the door, but it didn't budge against his strength. That worried him. She was stuck here in the middle of town, without neighbors and without a phone. Without protection.

She needed more than a fairy godmother. She needed someone to keep her safe. He couldn't drive off and leave her here alone. No sirree, no self-respecting Oglethorpe would do such a thing. And if there were one thing he had in abundance, it was self-respect.

"Bye, Sam!"

"You aren't turning down an offer of free labor, are you?" He pushed the door wide open. "Why don't you turn on the lights? You look like a ghost." Or was it shock? Rubbing his hand along the wall, he found the switch, but nothing happened. "Don't you have the power turned on?"

Ellie inhaled a deep breath. "I didn't have a chance to get the power transferred to my name before I left for

New York." She stepped back into deeper shadows. "I'll call first thing tomorrow."

Sam's senses went on alert. Whether she liked it or not, that marriage ceremony made this his business. Even a temporary fake wife deserved his protection.

"Yeah, you do that." He didn't try to hide his annoyance. "For now, grab your stuff."

"What?" Ellie couldn't help her shriek. So, the place was a little dusty. And the lights weren't connected. What business was it of his? "Hey, put that dress back!"

"You aren't staying here without electricity or a phone." Sam jerked the gold garment bag out of her reach. "Let's go."

"Who do you think you are?" Ellie grabbed at the dress bag. "Give me that dress."

Sam heard the panic in her voice. Yep, get the dress and this little lady would follow. "I'm the man you married, remember?"

"Come on, Sam," Ellie backed off. "I feel silly wrestling over a garment bag." Tilting her head, she grinned. "You know that ceremony was a sham."

"So is the idea of you staying in this place." Cool resolve and determination rang out with each word. In shadowy light, he saw her frown.

What should he do? He didn't want to leave her here, but she was one determined female. Just then his stomach growled so loud that Ellie laughed. Relieved, he joined in.

Sam tried for a teasing tone. "Come on, woman.

Can't you tell you're dealing with a starving man?" He nodded toward her bags. "Grab that stuff and bring it along. It'll be safer in the truck."

Hunger pangs twisted through Ellie's stomach as she tried to resist his offer. Food sounded good. Who was she kidding, anyway? The thought of spending the night alone in this dark building, without a bed or telephone, gave her the creeps.

Not for the first time, she questioned her decision to give up her garage apartment. But she had a plan. A person had to dream, didn't she? Shrugging, she grabbed her bags and locked the door while Sam stashed her things in the back of his truck.

"This is good." Ellie took another bite of cheeseburger and dabbed a napkin at the juice running down her arm. "You didn't have to come back, you know."

Sam lifted a shoulder. With his mouthful of burger, he didn't try to answer. What had possessed her to move into that place, anyway? Even now, he could still see shadows in her eyes.

A satisfied feeling rolled over him as he watched her devour the last of the fries. Oh, yeah, she was starving. He was glad his conscience had made him check on her one more time. This delayed his return home, but he was eating with the best-looking woman in the restaurant. How could he argue with that?

When they finished, he suggested a stop by the local discount store. "Don't you need this?" Sam held up a brand-name window cleaner. Ellie had a lot of scrubbing to do.

She reached past him for the store brand. "This works just as well."

There were several items in her basket. He watched as she did a swift tally and then put some things back on the shelf. He snapped his mouth shut. She would have been better off asking for money for their little acting job, instead of a wedding dress. How did she plan to survive until her first customers appeared?

"I'm ready to go, if you are." Ellie looked past his shoulder, avoiding eye contact.

Sam waited on the other side of the checkout, so she wouldn't feel he was snooping. He had guessed all he needed to know. "I'll carry that." He took the bag out of her hand. One bag? Who went to Swift-Mart and left with one bag? Who was she trying to kid? "Anywhere else you want to go?"

"No, thanks." She glanced around the dark parking lot, and turned to Sam. "Um . . . maybe I should go back and pick up a flashlight and some candles."

Sam half-lifted her into the truck seat and slammed the door. It was all he could do to keep control of his temper. How did she expect to live? "You won't need candles after tomorrow." He climbed in and started the engine. He stared at her shadowy face in the dim light of the cab. "You are having the power turned on tomorrow, aren't you?"

Back off, Sam. He tried to get a grip on his emotions. It was concern for her that made him angry, but she didn't know that. He didn't want her to think he was trying to take over her life. But there was only so much a man could overlook.

Taking a deep breath, he wheeled the truck into the highway without waiting for her answer. He didn't like throwing his weight around, but he was going to stick his neck out one more time. Taking a quick right, he pulled into the motel parking lot beside the restaurant where they'd eaten supper.

"Hang on a second. I want to be sure I can get a room."

Ellie hated the way her eyes clung to his retreating figure. She could still feel the heat from his touch when he'd helped her into the truck. Even in the green glow from the parking lot lights, Sam looked strong and capable. The easy way he carried himself, from the long-legged stride to the swing of his shoulders, made her feel . . . safe. That wasn't a feeling she'd had often in her life.

Always in the back of her mind one thought remained constant. If her parents had left her on the church steps, they could come back for her at any time. Right? That's how she'd lived her life, one day at a time. After meeting Sam, she wanted more.

Sam slid onto the leather seat and started the engine. "No problem." He pulled the truck around to the end of the building. "Let's take a look."

Ellie tried to hide the hitch in her breath as he helped her out of the truck. Excitement rushed over her from the touch of his hand on her arm. *You have to stop this*, she berated herself silently as she followed in his steps.

Sam flicked on the room light, causing her to blink.

Two double beds, the same as before. Something inside her brain clicked.

"You were planning to spend your vacation in New York." The evasive dart of his glance was her answer. "Why did you do it, Sam?"

She couldn't afford another night in a motel. Better to have it out with him now. She couldn't let him keep doing things for her. She didn't want him to suspect how close to the edge she was pushing her finances— or her emotions. Every minute she spent in his company was one more minute she had to fight a growing attraction to him.

It would be nice to have someone like Sam in her life, someone she could depend on. But that was out of the question. Once he left town, her life would be as empty as before. A wave of sadness washed over her. Having someone dependable, someone to share life with, seemed like a dream. It was what she wanted more than she had realized.

Could she have that dream? For a second, she tried to imagine being part of a family. What would it be like to belong to a family like Sam's?

He checked out the bathroom. "This looks good, don't you think?" He ignored the way she stood with her hands on her hips, her mouth twisted in a tight-lipped expression that made her look like she'd just eaten a lemon. "Let's get our bags."

"I'm not staying here."

Sam stopped midway through the door and turned to face the accusing tone in her voice. Okay, so he had expected some resistance. Couldn't she see he just wanted to help?

"Why make a big deal out of this? You expect me to go back to that shop and sleep on the floor?" He shrugged as if he could care less, but he felt stiff just from the thought of sleeping on a hard floor. "Okay, if that's what you want." He noted her startled reaction. "I thought you'd like a shower, maybe a chance to wash your hair. Women always want to wash their hair."

"I don't expect you to sleep on the floor," she mumbled, scuffing the toe of her shoe in the carpet. "You can stay here." She glanced toward the door. "Will you take me back, please?"

"You're the boss." Sam motioned her out. He noticed the glitter of tears in her eyes. "Let's go." Shadows darkened her eyes to a deep forest-green. So what was new? She'd had shadows in her eyes in the restaurant. Something else must be bothering her.

"You don't have to stay with me at the shop."

"Whither thou goest—"

"Sam! You know that ceremony wasn't real."

Sam clutched at his heart and managed a lovesick expression that teased a grin to her lips. When Ellie giggled, he realized that's what he'd been waiting for, for her to look less tense, less scared. Why?

Realizing where his thoughts were headed brought him to his senses. Sam stopped the clowning. His face grew stern. "It's your choice, Ellie." For long seconds he watched her expressions change like flashes on a TV screen. It didn't take a fairy godmother to tell him that she didn't want to spend the night sleeping on the floor any more than he did. "I stay where you stay."

"That's not fair." She stomped her foot, then giggled at the startled look on Sam's face that mirrored her own reaction. "I haven't done that in years." Her expression sobered. "This isn't your problem, Sam."

Hands on hips, copying her earlier stance of objection, Sam stared at her, ripping her argument to shreds without saying a word.

Why did he have to be this way? Strong, honorable, likeable, everything she'd ever dreamed a man could be. And the last thing she could have in her life. It wasn't fair to ask him to sleep on a hard floor, when two very comfortable-looking double beds were within touching distance.

She hadn't asked him to rent the room. This was his idea, though she admitted she felt safer here with him than back in the dark, lonely building on Main Street.

That was part of her problem. When she was with Sam, she felt safe. That made her more uneasy than she wanted to admit, even to herself. "I can't stay in this motel with you. I live in this town. Can't you see?"

"What?"

"People might get the wrong idea. This is a small town, you know. Once people make up their minds about something, it's awfully hard to change their opinion."

"You're worried about your reputation?" Sam watched color flood her face. "You stayed with me in a motel last night. What's different now?"

"I didn't know anyone." Ellie edged toward the door. She tried to keep her eyes from darting to the bathroom door. She was wavering, but it would be better if they left, no matter how much she'd like to make use of the shower . . . and that soft-looking bed.

"My guess is you don't know many people in this town." His words ricocheted off the walls and into Ellie's heart.

Dread washed over her as she accepted the truth of his words. Okay, so she had spent her life in Asheboro. But that was the only tie she had to this town. A chill caused the hair on her neck to stand up.

"What are you saying?" Heart pounding, she stepped back as he turned, his broad shoulders filling the door. His nearness held her speechless. "I grew up in this town."

"And if the old ladies who raised you were as protective of you as I think they were, you didn't get out much. Did you?"

"Okay! You win. We'll stay here." Ellie charged past him to get her bags from the truck. Anything was better than hashing out the barren recollections of her childhood. "I would love a shower." Never mind that she wanted to forget the memories his words brought back.

Could that be the reason Sam's protective attitude got around her defenses? Was she starving for attention, or was it just Sam? She felt indebted to him. That didn't sit well with her at all. She didn't want to feel anything for him.

"Why don't you get a shower first?" She watched as

he tried to hang her dress on the short hook in the closet. He looked over his shoulder, one eyebrow raised. "I'd like to wash my hair and . . . soak awhile, if that's all right with you?"

"Sure," Sam grunted. "That sounds like a good plan." He turned from the garment bag and reached for his shaving kit. "I won't be long."

Ellie barely had time to sort through her meager selection of clothing and get her toiletries before he came back in the room . . . half-naked! Well, he had on jeans, but they were unsnapped at the waist. And if that wasn't enough to start her heart racing, he had left off his shirt, exposing enough muscled chest to cause a girl to swoon.

Drops of moisture glistened in dark hair still wet from his shower. Manly scents of aftershave and soap drifted around her as she stared at the towel he alternately rubbed on his head and chest. Her wayward gaze settled on his broad, tanned, masculine chest.

"You can have the bath." His face fell into that special grin that slipped past her defenses. "Use all the water you want!"

The warmth of his smile would have dried her hair if she'd been the one just out of the shower. But since she wasn't, she felt the power of his charm singe her skin.

"Thanks!" She choked as she turned sideways to slip by him without making body contact. It wasn't enough. Across the room, his scent had been tantalizing. Up close, she could feel the heat of his body, smell the all-male aroma of his aftershave, and see the glint in his eyes.

He knew! With a startled gasp, Ellie jerked her eyes from his and stumbled through the bathroom door.

Drat the man! She panted as she fell back against the closed door. He'd noticed her reaction to his lack of clothing. Okay, so he'd been half-dressed. If the half she'd seen had affected her this bad, she doubted she'd survive if she ever saw him . . . in swim trunks.

An hour later, wishing it could have been longer, Ellie strolled back into the room as if nothing had happened. Nothing had. Except her heart had nearly pounded out of her body, while her blood had reached a temperature hotter than any water faucet could deliver.

But she was calm now. She had soaked until the water cooled. When she couldn't stand the chill any longer, she had run another tubful of hot water. Now she was squeaky clean and as wrinkled as a prune, but she could handle this. After all, this wasn't the first time she'd spent the night in the same room with Sam.

"I was about to send out a search party." His eyes sparkled with laughter as he waved a slice of pizza toward the box on the dresser. "Have some pizza." He took a bite out of the slice in his hand. "I started craving pepperoni."

Ellie's tension melted away as the warmth of Sam's grin wrapped around her. A pang twisted her stomach. She was starving. How could that be? Did the fact that Sam's chest was covered by a navy T-shirt give her back her appetite?

"It smells wonderful." She poured Pepsi over the cup of ice he'd left for her.

"It's good."

"Mmmmmm." She was safer if she kept her mouth full. Not that she'd have that problem, with pizza sitting around the room. "Sam?"

"Mmm?"

"Why did you leave New York? Earlier than you planned, I mean?" Her glance dared him to tell the truth.

Sam wadded up a napkin and threw it across the room toward the trash. He should have guessed she wouldn't let this drop. He'd been around her long enough to recognize that determined gleam in her eyes.

Her eyes had started his troubles. When she smiled, they sparkled like green jewels. Something about the glimmer in her eyes and her smile reminded him of all the things missing from his life. Ellie did that to him without even trying. She made him want things he tried to ignore.

He couldn't tell her he felt Shawn and Dawn had taken advantage of her. She was happy she had gotten the wedding dress for her efforts. But what was that designer dress worth in Asheboro? She'd been in New York City, trying to get home with an overstuffed garment bag and little else. She deserved more. He hated the idea that the famous couple had used Ellie, just as his grandfather had been used.

For as long as he could remember, he had vowed to carry his own weight in this world. He never intended to be indebted to another human being as long as he lived. But Shawn and Dawn owed Ellie, and as a member of Shawn's family, Sam felt responsible.

But what kept gnawing at his gut was the knowledge that he owed her too. If she hadn't agreed to take part in the fake ceremony, he wouldn't have the chance to buy his land.

She didn't need to know that. The less she knew about him, the better. He didn't want her gratitude. From what he had seen of Miss Emiline Anastasia Gray, she had a bushel of pride.

"The truth?"

Ellie stopped chewing and raised startled eyes. He had his back turned, but he watched her in the mirror. She glanced to his reflection. Sam held her mirrored gaze. After a long beat, their eyes glued to each other's reflections, she nodded. His tension relaxed a notch. Picking up a slice of pizza, he turned back to perch on his bed.

"I wanted to take a look at the land Shawn promised to sell." *Sounds good, Sam.*

"So, why are you staying in Asheboro?" Ellie forced a casual tone. His searching glance had almost caused her heart to stop beating. She wasn't sure how she knew, but she felt in her bones that he wasn't telling her the truth.

She wanted to know the real Sam, to know what he was hiding. The admission scared her. She wanted to know everything about Sam Oglethorpe.

Sam refilled his glass, added more ice, took a long swallow, and topped up his glass again. Man, pizza made him thirsty. What was he supposed to say now?

"Yeah, well, I've been thinking about that." He turned a serious face toward her. "While you were in the tub, I had an idea." He took a deep breath. "Why don't you come home with me for a few days?"

"What?" Someday, she hoped, she would outgrow that awful habit. Blurting out the first thing that came to her head had always been her problem. According to the elderly sisters, it was a burden she would bear the rest of her life, if she didn't learn some self-restraint.

Of course, the elderly ladies had known all about willpower. To their credit, they had done their best to instill the idea of restraining emotions in Ellie. Not that she'd been averse to learning self-control, but she still had problems putting the idea into practice. This time she felt her reaction was justified.

Go home with Sam? See his house? Learn about his life? Did she dare? How could she say goodbye if she got to know him better? How could she say goodbye now?

"Thanks . . . but . . . I can't."

"Why?" Sam swallowed the lump of pizza that lodged in his throat. Had he lost his mind? Why was he asking her to spend more time with him? "Don't you want to see the land that started all this trouble in the first place?"

She'd gotten under his skin enough already. Why was he pushing her to spend more time with him? Didn't he have a lick of sense? "You would have a safe place to stay while you wait for the utility companies to do their work."

And the truth was out. Sam realized that his protective instincts were on the warpath. He had no control over his tongue or his feelings. Shucks, if he were honest with himself, he didn't want to take back his offer.

That fact frightened him more than his need to take care of her. To think he wanted this stranger, his partner in a make-believe marriage, to see his pride and joy terrified him. His gut twisted, forcing air from his lungs as he waited for her to respond.

"I can't," Ellie said as she focused on the last of her drink. She didn't dare accept his invitation. He was everything she had dreamed about in a man. If she went with him, visited his home, his life, she was afraid she'd never recover.

"I-I-I have to stay here to make contacts. Unlock the doors, and . . . and . . ." She cast him a look that bordered on panic. Her need to be with him, to get to know him better, went against every plan she had made. "I can't."

Sam lifted the remote and clicked on the movie channel. With any luck he could find a comedy, something to change the atmosphere in the room. He needed a chainsaw to slice through the tension. Short of that, he'd find a funny movie.

"I bet you're glad to get rid of this garment bag," Ellie said as Sam hung the gold dress bag in her shop the next morning. They had managed to get through breakfast without mishap. In a mutual effort to keep things impersonal, they had strayed to childhood stories.

Sam told her about his first unsupervised attempt to make pancakes. When he realized he was showing her a side of life that she'd never been able to experience, his words had stopped in mid-sentence.

Her upbringing in the strict confines of the old

ladies' house had been limited. But she was a survivor. Sam needed to learn that fact.

She rescued the moment by laughing at the picture of him as a ten-year-old, covered in drops of batter, trying to cook his first pancakes. While she laughed, her heart had twisted in a bittersweet pain. She longed to see her children experience the kind of love parents could give. But lately, her visions were filled with a child who favored Sam.

Shocked at what her thoughts implied, Ellie babbled out the story about cooking the elderly sisters' favorite rooster. By the time they stopped laughing, their appetites had returned.

Now Sam was unloading her things from his truck for the last time. Saying goodbye was the part she hated. Would she ever see him again? Would he think about her?

Guilt washed over her. She'd spent way too much energy thinking about Sam after he left the first time. Now his leaving hurt more. They had shared memories from their past. The more she learned about him—like how his eyes sparkled when he laughed, or that they turned dark, almost brown, when he was angry or serious—the more she would miss him.

For one delicious moment, she wondered if he would kiss her goodbye. But after seconds of breathless anticipation, she blinked away the dreams and forced herself to face facts. All she was to Sam was a burden wished on him by his hapless cousin.

"Don't forget, Shawn wants us to go out to dinner sometime after the honeymoon." Even as he reminded her of Shawn's invitation, he cautioned, "But he doesn't always follow through on his plans."

"That sounds like fun." She planned to be too busy to accept any invitation. The less she saw of Sam, the less risk to her heart. Not that she believed in broken hearts. But the ache in her chest made her wonder. "I'm not sure I want to be the center of another media circus."

"Don't worry." Sam grinned as he set her bags down. "Movie stars have a way of slipping off when they want some privacy." His dry tone implied what Ellie had already suspected: his famous cousin and his fiancée wanted *some* of the media attention. Still, if things hadn't gotten out of hand with reporters, she wouldn't be the proud owner of a Sae Wong original, either.

"You know how to get in touch if you need me?" He held her gaze with a steady look as he paused by the truck.

Her heart tap-danced in her chest as Sam's gaze dropped to her lips. Would he kiss her, one last time? Even as her breath caught, he leaned near. As her heart pounded against her ribs, she felt his warm lips brush her cheek.

Disappointment weighed on her. As if tired of dancing at high speed, her heart slowed. Dragging in a gulp of much-needed air, she forced a smile to lips that wanted to cry as he stepped away.

"You will call?"

His concern and the serious expression on his face were almost more than she could take. Why couldn't he see her as a woman, instead of as another responsibility? She sighed, determined he'd never know that she dreamed of more.

"Yes, I'll call," she repeated, then laughed past the sadness filling her heart. It wouldn't do to let him see how she felt. "Thanks for everything." Forcing a grin, she waved. As the black vehicle pulled out of sight, she felt dampness on her cheeks.

Another goodbye, but this one hurt more than she would have dreamed possible.

What was she thinking? When had she leaned on anyone for support? It was bad enough that she'd accepted Sam's help last night. And on the ride home from New York. And the first night they spent in a motel. The list went on and on.

How had this happened?

Chapter Five

W hen the truck crested the hill, Sam took his foot off the gas pedal, allowing the pulsing throb of the engine to ease into a comforting hum as he stared straight ahead.

Nestled in the rolling foothills of the Blue Ridge, Pilot Mountain stood like a beacon. One glance told Sam he was home.

He felt a connection to the early inhabitants of the area as he looked at the majestic shape. After feasting his eyes on the natural landmark, he dropped his gaze to the old house nestled in the lower ridge of the mountain.

Looking at the house that had been his grandfather's inheritance until that ill-fated poker game filled Sam with a pride so fierce it threatened to choke him. His roots were buried deep in this land. Five years ago, Shawn had admitted he had no interest in living in the "sticks" and had sold him the old house. All that was missing from the original family holdings was the surrounding land. Soon, Sam would hold the deed.

Sam relaxed his grip on the steering wheel and willed the tension from his body. Always, when he thought of what his grandfather had loved and lost, his heart filled with anger.

He knew pride fueled his emotions. When he let himself relax, he admitted there was a target for his anger. Not his grandfather, not his grandfather's brother, not even Shawn, the cousin who spent summers and holidays in the old house that should have belonged to Sam's grandfather.

His anger was focused on the weakness that wouldn't let his grandfather refuse a dare.

Sam had promised himself that as the last of the Oglethorpes, he would regain possession of the property that belonged to his family.

Oh yeah, he knew what it was like to want something so bad you'd do anything to get it. Sweat broke out on his forehead. His gut twisted. He could hear Ellie's voice chasing around in his head like bits of a song. How could she make him forget everything he had worked for? Even for a day?

This was what he'd wanted from the time he first heard the story when he was ten. He dreamed of reclaiming the family land.

When he had bought the house, his goal had taken on new life. But Shawn knew about that fateful card game too, and he refused to sell the land—until now. When he realized that Sam was the only man who could help him pull off his plans for a private wedding, Shawn made his offer.

Sam squinted against the glare of the late morning sun, put the truck in gear, and let his foot ease off the clutch. As the tires crunched down the graveled drive, his heart swelled with pride. He was coming home to Oglethorpe House.

He would have helped with the fake wedding even without Shawn's offer to sell this land. Blood was thicker than water, in his book. He wouldn't have let Shawn down. But he didn't refuse the offer, either.

So why had Shawn turned his offer into a repetition of the past? His dare made this situation as underhanded as the bet their grandfathers had made. That question twisted Sam's insides into knots while the truck rolled toward the house.

Up close, he could see faded paint peeling from the walls, hinting at years of neglect. Some of the imperfections were hidden in shadows cast by the midday sun.

Overgrown rosebushes and shrubs joined the majestic old oak trees that shadowed the sparse grass of the neglected lawn. Everything about the house, the rockers on the porch, the rose bushes, hinted of happier days.

Sam's heart swelled. One paint stroke at a time, he planed to restore this property.

Now if he could just get Ellie Gray out of his mind. He'd spent more time thinking about the substitute bride than he wanted to admit. Even with his eyes glued to the old walls of peeling paint, he was thinking about her. What would she think of the house?

Parking beside the crumbling sidewalk, he headed

inside. He had to stop thinking about Ellie. There was no time in his life for a green-eyed vixen. He had responsibilities.

Stepping through the front door, he breathed in the lingering odor of furniture polish. Soaking up the essence of his surroundings, he watched particles of dust dance in the sunlight spilling through the windows. When he moved to close the door, his boots echoed on the wood floors. The dull emptiness of the sound repeated in the thud of his heart.

For the first time since he'd acquired the house, his joy at owning the building dimmed. Today, the walls were just walls, not a frame supporting the roof over generations of his ancestors. The honed wood floors were just boards, scarred and gouged . . . like his heart. How had his life come to this?

Shaking his head in disgust, Sam dropped his bag and headed for the kitchen. He needed about a gallon of coffee and some food. This foolishness would stop when he filled his stomach. Maybe work would help him forget the green eyes that haunted him. He had to get Ellie out of his head.

Until he had the deed to this land, he had nothing to offer a woman. Especially someone searching for a real home, like Ellie.

After calling the utility company, Ellie's first priority was picking up her cat. Her former landlady had promised to feed the black and gray striped cat on the condition that Ellie remove the big tom as soon as she returned from New York.

Like most cats, Benny had his own schedule. While he checked in most evenings, she had no idea where he spent his time. Only the dead carcasses on her doorstep gave her the hint that he spent much of his time hunting.

Ellie accepted what all cat lovers knew: they didn't own their pets, the cats consented to live with them. With that knowledge, Ellie parked in her old space beside the garage.

On the count of three, just like clockwork, her former landlady stuck her head of white curls out the backdoor.

"Ellie? How was your trip?"

"Hi, Miss Margaret, the trip was good. How are you? Have you seen Ben?"

"Come on in, child. I told you not to worry about that monster of yours." She stepped back for Ellie to enter. "He's been here, off and on." Closing the door, she motioned Ellie toward the kitchen. "Thank goodness you're back. He started leaving his little surprises on my doorstep."

"Oh, Miss Margaret, that's so sweet." Ellie giggled.

"Sweet?" The elderly woman's voice rose with pretended annoyance. "Finding a dead smelly little carcass on the top step is sweet?" The spry little woman waved Ellie to a chair and started pouring the expected cup of tea. "I have to admit, I'm glad you're home." Twinkling blue eyes glinted over her glasses. "Much more digging to bury the presents Ben leaves and I'd be too tired to play bridge."

Ellie laughed as her landlady intended. They both

knew nothing short of a major crisis would keep the feisty senior from her card game.

"You're feeling well, then?"

"Fair to middling. Except for this old arthritis, I can't complain." The watery eyes squinted across the table. "Is it my imagination or have you lost weight, child?"

"Mmm . . ." Ellie took a quick sip of tea. "I may have walked off a pound or two. It's easier to walk in New York than to wait for a taxi."

"Don't run yourself into the ground. You'll make yourself sick."

"I'm fine, really." Ellie searched for a topic to distract her neighbor's eagle eyes. "I'm sorry Ben's little thank-you presents made your doorstep smell."

"He's a fine hunter, that boy." Miss Margaret pretended to dislike Benny, but Ellie had often caught the elderly woman rubbing him when she thought Ellie wasn't looking. "Too bad he has to go after the birds."

"I know," Ellie sighed. Their one bone of contention was over Ben catching songbirds from the back yard. Though Ellie could have found other places to live that were less drafty and more convenient, Ben and her landlady had kept her settled for the past six years. Now she was uprooting herself, and her cat, for who knew what?

"I don't think he'll like living in my new place." Oops! Ellie jumped to her feet, panicked by the urge to ask if she could move back. She couldn't give up now—she just couldn't. "Speaking of which, I need to run! I have to grab Ben and get back to work. Miss Margaret, you take care, now."

The door slammed behind her as she dashed out. That was close. She had almost slipped up and asked for her old apartment back. She couldn't give up now. She had to prove she could make it on her own.

"El-lieee?"

She stopped the mad dash toward the garage. Why did Miss Margaret sing out her name as if she were calling the cows home? "Yes?"

"I meant to tell you, I'm moving in with my nephew, Jim."

"Oh!" Ellie's stomach clenched. "I know your family's been after you to make the move for a good while." She didn't have a choice now. "When did you decide?"

"After you left, I got mighty lonesome. Jim and his wife live across town. He convinced me I don't need to live alone when I have family nearby. And his wife's a good cook." The old lady wheezed as she laughed.

"You'll enjoy the company." Ellie reached to hug the elderly woman. Her weak moment, the idea of giving up and moving back, wouldn't have worked anyway. Just as well.

"You'll know where to find me. Take care now, you hear!"

Ellie spent the rest of the morning working her worries out in a frenzy of cleaning. By noon she was less optimistic and more tired. The front windows sparkled. But no matter how hard she scrubbed the floors, the dark stains were there to stay. Little by little, her options for arranging displays in the room diminished.

The walls were a nightmare, covered with a brownish-pinkish color that made her feel sick. How could fabrics or her finished designs look good against that moldering backdrop? Painting was out of the question. The place was too big and paint too expensive.

She was ready for a break. Worry and work had used up her energy. A quick check of her watch brought a big sigh. Sam had left four and a half hours ago, but it seemed like forever. She couldn't look anywhere without seeing his grin. How could a man she had known for such a short time invade her life like this?

Heads turned when he walked into a room. But he was more than just a good-looking guy. He was kind and caring; look at the way he made sure she got home safely. No wonder she missed him.

Okay, she was being silly. So he kissed like a dream! She didn't have time to waste on a guy. No matter how much Sam made her heart churn—she had to think about survival.

As a quivering breath escaped, she couldn't help but wonder if she would see him again. Then her real panic began. She'd spent the morning thinking about Sam instead of making plans for her business. She needed to get her mind off Sam and back on her plans for the shop.

Things were more complicated than she'd expected. Hands on hips, she glanced around the large, disorganized room. The flaws in her plan jumped out at her.

She didn't have the necessities. Her bank balance was as flat as roadkill. She could manage without a place to cook. But to run a business, she would need a phone—

A loud pounding on the front door interrupted her depressing thoughts. Rushing to see who was trying to knock the door down, she found herself wishing she had planned this out better.

The face staring at her through the front door wiped every thought from her head, stopped her heart in mid-beat, and brought a flush to her face.

"Sam?" She twisted the lock, hoping the glass door prevented him from hearing the excited tone in her voice. "What are you doing here?" One hand on her hip, she tried for a casual tone. "Did you change your mind about going home again?"

"I went home." Sam barreled past her. The thud of his boots on the wood floor echoed in the empty room. "For thirty minutes." He whirled, nearly knocking her down with his elbow.

"What are you doing back here?"

Sam whipped folded papers out of the back pocket of his jeans and waved them like a flag. "This came . . . special delivery!"

She felt the spatter of his hiss. Why was she standing so close? From the minute he stepped in the door, she had been on his heels like a flea on a hound dog.

Inching back a step, she studied the grim expression on his face. "What is it?"

"It's from Shawn." His eyes glittered with emotion. His shoulders heaved under a worn T-shirt that enhanced the green of his eyes.

"What?" She sounded like a broken record, but on the trip, he'd seemed laid-back, dependable—nothing like the raging male now in front of her eyes.

His chest heaved. The cords in his neck stood out. Muscles in his jaw rippled as if a snake were crawling under his skin. Every inch of his body shouted power, male strength, and . . . allure.

Despite the storm warnings in his eyes, the sight of him kept her speechless. This was the kind of man she wanted by her side in case of trouble.

Had Shawn gone back on his word? What else could have Sam this riled?

She admired Sam's determination to regain his heritage. He cared about his family and his roots. All the things she didn't have. Oh, yeah, she could appreciate his feelings, unlike people who took family for granted. She reached a tentative hand for the papers he clenched in his fist.

"Let me see."

He shoved the papers in her hand. "You're going to love this!"

She gave the papers a quick glance. "What . . . what does this mean?" Her hands trembled as she stared at the man in front of her. "What is this?"

"Shawn's up to his old tricks!" Sam leaned down, his

nose almost touching hers as he stabbed a furious finger at the papers in her hand. "He wants me to throw a big reception for the happy couple!" He twisted away with a groan that had Ellie reaching out to ease his pain. "At my house."

"But . . . I thought . . . they . . ." Taking a calming breath, she started again. "I thought Shawn and Dawn were going on a honeymoon—"

"They are!" Sam swung back to face her, disgust written on his face as if someone had used a permanent marker. "When they get back, he wants a big party, before he'll sign over the deed."

"Why?"

"When we signed the papers at the wedding—remember? After the . . . kiss?" Sam refused to let his mind go there.

Ellie nodded. Oh, she remembered, all right. "A close blunder, we didn't know we were supposed to fake the signing."

"Right! Well, thanks to Shawn's tricks, we signed a contract agreeing to the details!"

"It isn't possible. It can't be."

"Well, I'm on your side, babe! But according to this letter from Shawn—"

"It's a joke, right?"

"He had the letter notarized! It's real."

"It can't be!"

Sam frowned at the note of panic in her voice. What was wrong with her? Something didn't seem right. He'd expected her to be shocked, but . . .

"You aren't losing it, are you?"

"No!" She whirled away, not wanting him to see how much this upset her. Not twenty minutes ago, she realized how unrealistic her plan was, now this. "It's just—"

"This changes everything, you know."

"Why?" She blinked to clear the confusion from her head. "What's different now?"

"That's just the point." Clenched fists braced on the door frame, Sam stared out the front door. "Nothing is different. The house isn't ready for visitors."

"You can hire someone to help."

"Right, but that takes time and money." Sam glared at her chalk-white face. "I can't spare the time right now. Can you?"

"Me?" Ellie answered past the lump in her throat. She couldn't afford to eat. "No!"

"I'm so close to closing this deal. I can't give up now."

Ellie wanted to argue, but it was no use. She heard the anguish in his voice. She knew how much this land deal meant to him. "What are we going to do?"

Sam shrugged powerful shoulders as he turned away. He didn't want to lay this on her, but they might as well get it over with. "I need your help to get the house ready."

She started shaking her head. "I can't—"

"Look, Ellie, we didn't plan this—"

"Don't you see?" She turned silver-green eyes on him as she waved toward the room. Sam had noticed her eyes changed color with her emotions, but now the green looked like a frozen lake. "I can't take the time."

"Look! This wasn't my idea either." His voice thundered in the vacant room. "Sorry . . ." He flung a hand in her direction. "I just thought . . . you might help—"

"I can't!"

"Why not? You helped Shawn and Dawn." The force of his voice rattled the windows. He hadn't meant to raise his voice again. But if this land deal fell through, he lost everything—the chance to buy the land and contact with the woman facing him like a bull terrier.

It shocked him to realize how much he wanted to keep Ellie in his life, how much his reactions to Shawn's letter were motivated by the need to look out for her.

"Look around you, Sam! I'm trying to start a business. This is my life!" It was the truth. But her real fear was spending more time with Sam. Her head knew better than to believe in dreams, but her heart was filled with hope. Everything she'd ever wanted stood glaring at her.

"This is my life too!" His words stabbed her like pins as he waved the papers in front of her face. "And if you remember, you signed on for this little prank just like I did."

"Not like this, I didn't." She turned a furious glare on him. "What I agreed to do in New York didn't hurt anyone. We helped two people have a little privacy for their wedding. What was wrong with that?"

"Nothing, Ellie! But things didn't work out as we planned. This isn't your fault or mine. But we agreed to take part in the fake wedding, now we have to control the damage."

"What damage?" Her body quivered like her voice,

but determination filled her. "Shawn and Dawn are off on their honeymoon, right? So what's the problem?"

Sam stepped so close his toes touched hers. She could feel heat radiating off him. His scent, a blend of aftershave and male that had been absent from her life for hours, tantalized her memory.

"I'll tell you who it hurts." He leaned down until their lips almost touched.

Ellie's tongue slipped out to moisten the parched skin of her mouth. Her body quivered with anticipation. Was he going to kiss her? His hazel eyes bored into hers, then dropped to her lips. Did she see him swallow? Was he remembering the wedding kiss? She was. She could still feel the touch of his lips on hers.

"It hurts me, Ellie, and you, if you don't want to be the main topic of gossip in the news." Sam let his gaze drop one more time to her lips, then dragged his eyes from her face.

Her lips were tempting, even when he was angry enough to spit nails. Besides, he liked looking at her. Even with his future hanging by a prayer, he wanted to trace every line in the face that haunted his dreams.

It was a charming face under that layer of dirt. A large patch of grime covered her left cheek and her nose, while the rest of her face was streaked. Under the dust, she looked pale.

"But—"

Gritting his teeth, he turned away from the temptation to taste her lips. "I won't have it, Ellie. I don't intend for my name to be dragged through the media when Shawn's plans fall through. I don't want to be in the top-ten countdown on some late-night talk show because I'm the country cousin who didn't know how to throw a wedding party for my movie star cousin." Shoulders heaving, he fought for control and lowered his voice. "I don't want strangers digging through my past, dragging out dirty laundry."

"But—"

Sam whipped around for one last attempt to sway her decision. With his left hand on the wall over her shoulder, he leaned into her body.

It was a mistake he wouldn't make again. The scent of her filled his nostrils. Muscles in his thighs tightened. Much more of this temptation, and he'd forget what he was angry about. He stared at the wall over her head and took a deep breath. Once his head was halfway clear of thoughts of Ellie, he dared to focus on her deep green eyes. Eyes offering the comfort he longed to claim.

"I don't want the past dug up. Tales of my grandfather's poker game have been thrown in my face all my life." Clenching his jaw, he squeezed his eyes shut. He didn't want to see pity in Ellie's gaze, or see how cute she looked with dirt on her face. "Look." His voice dropped to a whisper. "Can't you help me out with this? Just help me make the house presentable?"

He struggled to inhale as her lips parted . . . perfect for kissing. His shoulders heaved. With the release of air from his lungs, his emotions escaped. Looking into her darkening gaze, his mouth lowered to claim her lips in a movement as old as time.

Ellie's sigh filled the room.

In that instant, nothing existed for him but the woman filling his senses. The fierce beating of his heart, begging for his surrender to her power, brought him back to reality.

Releasing lips swollen from his kiss, Sam met her dazed gaze for a tension-filled moment. Then, sighing, he rested his forehead on hers. "Shawn can be a pain, but he's family."

Chapter Six

Family!

Ellie slumped against the wall, fighting the weakness in her knees and her heart. Kissing Sam made her want more than he was offering.

"At least you had a family." Her voice trembled. She could still feel the touch of his lips. Heat traveled to the deepest part of her, leaving a brand on her heart. She couldn't allow that! "That has to count for something."

"What are you saying?" Sam's head snapped back as if she had slugged him.

"Even if your grandfather dragged the family's name through the gossip mill, you know who you are." She straightened to her full height and met his puzzled look. She couldn't fault his surprised reaction. One minute she melted in his arms, the next she snapped off his head.

"Well—"

"I don't have a family." She aimed each word at his heart, jabbing at his chest with her index finger, knowing family was his weakness. Well, two could play this game. He had discovered her weakness and his power over her. This had gone far enough. It was one thing to marry him in a fake ceremony, but for her to drop everything to meet Shawn's demands was asking too much.

It meant losing her chance to start a business . . . and risking her heart. Her voice dropped to a whisper. "That's why I can't help you."

"I don't understand."

She ducked under his arm and moved out of his reach. He made her want things she couldn't have. Things she had to ignore, until she proved herself.

From across the room, she glanced back. "I can't help you." Her voice shook with emotion. "Working together that close . . . demands too much of a person. I-I don't have that extra—something, whatever it is—to give." She waved toward the room. "Don't you see? This empty shell is all I have. I don't have a choice. I have to make a success of this business. It's all I have."

She stared from her sewing machine to the box of sewing supplies she had unloaded from her car. "You know your roots as far back as settling that land." Her throat worked to get the words out. "My last name came from the dirty blanket I was wrapped in the night I was abandoned."

She darted a glance in his direction, hoping he wouldn't see the moisture in her eyes. "I don't know who my parents were, or who I am. I need to make a name for myself. Don't you see that, Sam? Can't you, of all people, understand?"

Her words touched a spot inside him that Sam hadn't known existed. He didn't have all the answers, but right now all he could think about was wrapping her in his arms and shielding her from the pain he heard in her voice.

He wanted to help her, keep her safe.

Neither of them moved for long seconds, yet he felt a sense of warmth surround him. "Okay." His breath escaped on a deep sigh. "We'll think of something."

Sam insisted on driving Ellie to pick up her cat. Now he glanced toward the passenger seat and watched the happy reunion between feline and woman. He could hear the large gray and black cat purring as she scratched behind his ears. A lump settled in his chest as he forced his attention back to the road. The muscles in his thighs tightened. He pictured Ellie's long fingers touching him with tenderness. Stop! Where had that come from?

He was getting in too deep. From the moment Ellie stared him in the eye and informed him she didn't have a family, he'd been lost. The attraction he'd felt for her before seemed nothing compared to the powerful emotions that filled him now. Even an hour later, he could still feel the urge to hold her close in his arms and protect her.

But he had been wrong about one thing. Emiline Anastasia Gray was not a damsel in distress. Not this girl, with her laughing green eyes and her way with people. She might be struggling now, but the word *distress* gave the wrong impression. Her inner strength made him feel weak.

He didn't want the woman who absorbed his every waking moment to live in that shop alone. He needed a solution, fast. He couldn't demand that Ellie drop everything and go with him. He felt responsible for her. He told himself it was because she had helped a member of his family. But the truth was that he couldn't get her out of his mind.

To make matters worse, he understood what drove her. He could appreciate her need to prove herself. But he didn't want to see her fail, either.

His determination to succeed had deep roots in his fear of failure. He felt a need to prove he was different from his grandfather, that he was a better person. He didn't want Ellie to have to face his climb to acceptance all over again.

Still, he couldn't lose sight of his goal, either. He was determined the Oglethorpe name would not be the focus of more gossip. His future depended on his success. He wanted a future. He wanted it all: a wife, children, and the homeplace that was his heritage.

He couldn't have either as long as the only thing he had to offer were the worn-out stories about a card game.

At this point, that special delivery letter from Shawn could ruin everything. That and the dare Shawn had made at the bachelor party.

No one knew of Shawn's taunt. If word got out about his part in the fake wedding, he'd be ruined. He hadn't worried at first. He just assumed the media attention was Shawn's problem. But now, all it would take was some reporter stumbling over the fact that he'd acted as the stand-in groom, and his future would become a nightmare reflection of his past.

He couldn't take a chance on that happening. He had to keep Shawn's dare a secret, even from Ellie. His grip tightened on the wheel. He hated the thought of deceiving her. It felt wrong.

Still, he couldn't risk new gossip that might follow his future like a dark shadow.

Escape from his past was so close. The future sparkled before his eyes like a rainbow. All the way home from New York, he'd had flashes of what his life would be like now that Shawn was willing to sell him the land.

Once that property was in his possession, he could shrug off the past. He could start over. He could look forward to a new generation of Oglethorpes . . . his children.

His wistful thinking wouldn't be worth a thing if he failed now. Shoulders heaving with a deep sigh, he parked the truck in front of Ellie's shop.

The outside looked better, he acknowledged. Ellie had polished the bay windows to a glossy shine. Colorful bundles of cloth added to a new look to the surroundings. Her sign, *Custom-made garments, alterations, and crafts by Ellie*, drew attention. The admission made him angry.

He swung the passenger door open and made a grab for the cat as the animal wiggled to get out of Ellie's arms. But she didn't need his help. With a move that showed long practice, Ellie wrapped her arms around the struggling feline. The big tom didn't show his claws, even as he pushed against her chest with his feet.

Sam's breath rasped through numb lips. He wanted to change places with the cat, to be the one receiving that hug. His lips spread in a reluctant grin as he recognized the struggle. He was under this woman's control as much as the cat in her arms. Yep, this struggle of wills had happened before.

Ellie crooned while she shifted to get a better grip on the squirming cat, and then slid out of the truck. Inside the door, she let Benny jump from her arms and watched as he explored the shop.

"Aren't you afraid he'll run away?" He felt weak just thinking of the struggle she'd fought and won. *If he knew what was good for him, he'd run, now! He would get in that truck and hightail it home. Let Ellie Gray take care of her own problems.*

Ellie brushed at her clothes and laughed as she followed Benny's progress around the room. "He will if the door is open." She nodded to the door Sam held and turned toward the back of the shop. "Everything is secure enough for him to be safe." She moved to double-check the back windows. "He needs to get acquainted with his new home." She watched Ben sniff around the workroom. "He'll be fine in a couple of days."

I wish I could say the same for myself, she thought as she reached for the broom.

Despite her brave words, the news that Sam needed her help to claim his land was playing tricks with her good sense. Probably because she'd spent way too much time fantasizing about him as she'd worked to clean up the shop. Memories of his hazel eyes and wicked grin had entertained her as she'd scrubbed and cleaned like Cinderella.

Okay, she knew Sam wasn't her Prince Charming. After all, she didn't have a wicked stepmother or step-sisters. She wished she did. At least then she'd have a family. Then Sam could be her Prince Charming. She darted a glance in his direction as he picked up some old boxes left by the previous tenant. Despite her grim thoughts, a smile tugged at the corners of her mouth. Sam would make a fine prince . . .

"What are you grinning about?"

"It isn't every day a girl has a hunk picking up her trash." Uh-oh, she didn't need to give him any ideas. But from the looks of that grin on his face, her self-reproach came too late.

Dimples slashed his cheeks. His eyebrows arched. "You think I'm a hunk?"

She gulped around the lump in her throat. He was a prince, all right. Look at the way he carried himself, straight and tall, with shoulders wide enough to carry the weight of the world. Yep, he was a hunk. But this line of thinking wasn't getting her anywhere. He couldn't suspect how important he'd become to her.

What self-respecting female would let a man know he'd interrupted her dreams from the moment they'd met? She managed a grin and winked.

"Any man who picks up trash for me is a hunk."

Sam's shrug was a masterpiece of suave muscle and motion as he turned away with a frown. "Figures!" He glared at the cat watching from a few feet away. "She's interested in my body, Ben, not my brain." Brows waggling, eyes sparkling with humor, he turned back to her. "Where do you want me to put the trash?"

Ellie laughed, despite the unnerving thoughts running through her head. He was fun to have around. She'd miss him when he left. "Beside the back door is fine." It hadn't been easy to say goodbye to him before. How could she send him away again, knowing how he affected her?

"Do you need me to hold the door?" Her voice rasped like a foghorn. What was she thinking? He had returned to ask for her help, not because he was interested in her. How could he be? She didn't have anything to offer a man like Sam. Fighting against the pain in her chest, Ellie dropped the broom and dashed for the back door.

She needed air.

How could she drop everything to go help him? He was all about family. She didn't even know her real name. How could she ignore this chance to start over? How could she pass up her chance to be somebody?

How could she refuse? Sam had showed her nothing but kindness from the moment they met. Despite the debate raging in her head, one thing remained clear. Sam's happiness was more important to her than she dared let him know.

She couldn't risk getting more involved with him.

Sam wasn't just any man. He had plans, a goal. He was driven just as she was. This was the worst possible time for her to start thinking about a man.

Not a man who could trace his family back to the first settlers. It was out of the question. Pushing the bolt, she slipped out the back door, careful even in her panic to prevent any escape attempt from Benny.

What was she going to do? After all this time, planning for her future, thinking of ways to make something of her life, and now this.

She was attracted to a man whose family history was as long as her leg. Worse, a man who needed her help to claim his heritage. Crossing the parking lot, she unlocked her car and stared at the contents. Her whole life was stashed in a Honda Civic. What did that say about her?

How could Sam think she would drop her plans for making a future? Slamming the door of the red car, she found herself wishing she could shut out her troubles as easily. Her hand trembled as she tried to fit the key in the lock. Nothing came easy.

All she had ever wanted was to be somebody.

She and Sam were complete opposites. He was trying to save what she hadn't been able to achieve in her twenty-six years, a place to belong. What a cruel joke fate had played on them. Sam had what she'd always dreamed of, but he needed her help to claim the very thing she wanted. And she had to refuse to help him.

Didn't she? How could she spend more time with the man she was starting to care about?

But her feelings for Sam demanded she help him out

of this situation. He cared about people, about family . . . all the things she wanted. How could she turn her back when he was trying to protect his family name?

His dedication to preserving family tradition touched something deep inside her. He was everything she wanted to be—loving, helpful, dedicated to family. All he asked was that she help get his house ready for Shawn and Dawn's wedding party.

If she refused, he would lose what she wanted most. How could she say no, even if helping him put her heart at risk? She believed in doing the right thing.

He could hire someone with more skill, she realized as she paced back and forth on the sidewalk behind the shop. But she needed a job—

"Anything I can do to help?"

Ellie stumbled on a crack in the pavement as his deep voice penetrated her troubled thoughts. "What?" She whirled to find him standing just a few feet away. "Oh, no, thanks," she said. Shoving the keys in her pocket, she turned to the car. "I was just . . . ugh . . . I can't decide whether to arrange the shop first, or get started with making samples . . . and unpack my supplies when I have time." It was the truth, even if that wasn't all she was stressing over as she stalked along the sidewalk.

"Ellie—"

"Sam—"

He laughed. The sound came from deep in his chest and wrapped around her. Her gaze strayed to that part of his body, then darted away. Why did he make her think about things she'd be better off ignoring? What was it about Sam Oglethorpe that made her want more . . . more than she'd had in her life before she met him . . . and more than she would have after he left?

"Okay, ladies first." His laughing glance reminded her that he was all male.

"I—"

"Let's get something to eat." He shrugged as their words came out at the same time again. She opened her mouth to refuse, but he said, "I haven't eaten all day."

Her stomach growled before she could think of an excuse. Okay, they could go eat. With other people around, she wouldn't notice him so much.

"I don't like leaving Benny alone in a new place."

"He'll be fine," Sam assured her as he pulled the truck into traffic. "Cats need the time to check out new territory."

"I hope he doesn't decide to spray everything."

"That wouldn't be good." Sam pulled into the Rockola parking lot. They walked in silence from the truck to the restaurant.

"I'm not very hungry," Ellie said as she slid into the booth the hostess indicated.

"Then pretend." Sam aimed a stern glare across the table as he picked up a menu.

"Why?"

"This is our first official meal as partners."

"Shh." Ellie darted a panicked glance around their booth. "Hey! I didn't agree to—"

"Aw, don't make me repeat all that again." Sam nodded toward the menu. "I'm starving." He grinned then added, "Besides, I take my responsibilities seriously."

"I am not your responsibility!"

Sam noted the gritted teeth, the flush that covered her clean face. Her hands clenched in fists on either side of the menu. Uh-oh, he'd made a blunder. Okay, he'd meant what he said. She didn't have to know what he was thinking.

"It was a joke." He glanced at the menu and struggled for inspiration on how to deal with Ellie's pride. "Lighten up. You're going to give me indigestion." He winked and waggled his brows. When her lips tilted up in a reluctant grin, his heart settled down to a regular pace.

But it was too late. He was in trouble. Truth was, he'd been in trouble from the moment that special delivery letter had arrived.

Nope, that was wrong. He'd been in trouble from the moment she stepped up beside him in front of the minister and started swishing the skirt of her wedding gown like a little girl. He could still see the smile of satisfaction that covered her face as she played with that wedding gown. Could he ever make her look that way?

"Okay, I'm having a cheeseburger," he said, ready for anything to get his mind off the woman facing him . . . the woman who had filled his head since the fake wedding.

When the food arrived, Sam frowned down at his plate and wished he were somewhere else. "I've been thinking. I have an idea for your business . . . and you'd be doing me a big favor." He kept his expression blank and met her startled green glance. "I'd pay, of course."

Her face flushed with color. "I said I'd help." She grabbed her glass of tea. "Isn't that enough?"

Sam toyed with his fork as an idea took shape in his head. This just might work. "Well, I need help. But, I thought, if your schedule is flexible enough, I . . . think you can help with my problem." That didn't sound too bad for something off the top of his head. Did it?

"What kind of help do you need?" Ellie almost choked on a piece of ice. Or was it the idea of spending time with Sam? What was he talking about? If he thought she would go along with the idea of leaving town, he could think again. "I'm not sure what you're asking."

"To tell you the truth, what I need is . . . a big job." Crossing his arms, Sam leaned on the edge of the table. "But maybe we'd better just forget I mentioned it." He settled back against the booth, as if putting more distance between them would erase his words.

"Oh no, you can't leave me hanging like that. You've made me curious, you have to explain." Forget curiosity. Sam had just handed her the best compliment a human being could receive. He'd asked for her help. He needed Ellie Gray's help.

Something inside her took off like a kite in a stiff breeze. A burst of confidence zinged through her, giving power to her growing determination.

Sam watched the flashing expressions crossing her face. What was she thinking? Her emerald gaze stuck to his face like metal to a magnet. At least he had her attention. It was all he could do to keep from grinning.

"It was a bad idea, okay." He fiddled with his glass as he glanced around for the waitress. "Are you ready to go?"

"Not until you tell me what you started to say." Ellie lifted her chin, daring him to try to make her leave the booth. "You helped me in more ways than I can count, Sam. Let me help you now."

Gotcha! Sam leaned back as he toyed with the glass. A note of fierce pride rang in Ellie's voice. If she suspected he was making this up, it would be all over. He couldn't let that happen. He couldn't leave her alone in this town.

"Okay, don't say I didn't warn you."

"I've been warned. What can I do to help you?"

"I need a decorator." Sam waited for her startled expression to ease. "But I don't have that kind of money. Especially with the land deal coming up." Her eyes glazed over as if he were speaking in a foreign tongue. "So, I wondered . . . since you don't have any customers . . ."

"Decorator?" Ellie blinked the cloud of confusion from her brain. Why was he asking her? Okay, so she worked with color and fabrics. But she wasn't trained.

She was lucky she knew anything about sewing. Most of the kids in her home economics classes hadn't pursued the skill. She wouldn't have either, if the old maid sisters hadn't forced her to practice after school. Everything the teacher assigned her to do in class, the sisters insisted Ellie repeat at home.

Moisture pooled in her eyes. She was grateful to the two women who had pushed her, who had forced her to learn a skill. It had taken her all this time to realize the elderly ladies had cared for her. Now she had to take care of herself. It was time she proved what she was worth.

But decorating Sam's house?

She needed a paying customer . . . any paying job was tempting. But she couldn't let herself get distracted by Sam. It wouldn't take much for her to lose her head and do something foolish. She'd been on the verge of feeling dizzy since he'd asked for her help.

All her life she'd wanted to belong, to count for something. To be needed by someone like Sam was almost as good.

"I'm not a decorator." The idea sent her into a fit of giggles. She'd never had a space to decorate. And who ever heard of an orphan learning the fine art of decorating? At the sight of Sam's worried gaze, she fought to hold back her laughter. "Hey, I can make curtains if that's what you want."

"You'll do it then?" Sam leaned across the table. "You'll go back with me? Make curtains for the house?" He settled against the cushioned softness of the booth. This was easier than he'd expected.

"But—"

"You need to be close by," he warned. "There are a lot of windows." He grinned at her look of confusion. "I know this is sudden, but I know a place in Redbud that would be perfect for you to open a shop."

Her heart raced. Thoughts tumbled through her head. "I'll come measure the windows." She couldn't turn down the first customer she had, or a chance to see more of Sam, could she?

"All I care about is making the house look like a home."

"How long have you owned this house?"

"About five years."

"Oh!"

Sam heard the unspoken question in her response. "I'm not trying to make you do something you'll regret. Redbud is a thriving little town. And the best news is that the town center is where the growth is, unlike most towns."

"Oh?"

Sam decided to ignore her. But then he heard himself say, "My office is small, but I'm only using one side of the building."

"What are you saying?"

"You could use the other side—"

"I'm not relocating, Sam."

". . . and there's a studio apartment upstairs." His brow arched, his lips twitched as he met her stormy gaze. "It would be perfect if you needed to sew late to meet a deadline . . . you wouldn't even have to leave the building." He grinned. "I wouldn't be your only customer, I promise."

Ellie choked something between a frustrated laugh and panic as she watched his very kissable lips widen in a grin that went straight to her heart. "You can't promise something like that!"

"Oh yes I can."

"I thought small towns were . . . shy of outsiders."

Sam grunted. "Believe me, their curiosity will outweigh their reluctance to accept you."

"I appreciate what you're trying to do, but—"

"What's keeping you here?"

"This is my hometown."

"You have relatives here? Friends?"

"No . . . well, Miss Margaret . . . but I grew up here."

"No offense, Ellie, but that's one of the best reasons I can think of for leaving."

"You didn't leave."

Sam looked into eyes a deep troubled green and frowned. "That's my point," he said with a sigh. "I don't want to see you make my mistake."

"Are you saying you wish you had moved away?"

"I'm saying I've had a rough time living up to expectations."

"Your business is successful."

"But at what cost?" Sam waved an arm. "Take a good look around you, Ellie. What would you lose if you left town today?"

Ellie's chin lifted. "This is home."

Sam knew the instant her chin tilted that he had lost the battle. He recognized a kindred spirit fueled by pride when he saw one. "I need to make a quick stop before we head back across town."

Ellie declined to go into the home improvement store with Sam. She needed to think. She needed a break. He filled her head with ideas she knew were impossible, but still . . .

When he laughed, her heart skipped with an excitement like nothing she had felt before. She liked the way he tilted his head when he laughed, and the way his eyes twinkled bright enough to light up her dreams.

Oh, yes, she needed a break from Sam. But she needed something else more. She needed work to make money. Sam was offering her a job. Not a small job, either. Making curtains for a twelve-room house would take time. She would make enough money to get on her feet.

But if she took the job, she would need to spend time at his house. Could she take the chance? He was right about relocating. Not just because of the job he offered, but about trying to make a future and forget the past.

Her unknown parents could be anyone she met on the street. It was enough to make her listen to his suggestion.

Every time she came face-to-face with anyone old enough to be her parent, she searched the stranger's face, looking for some sign of resemblance. Sam was right about one thing: starting over would give her a break. She'd been searching for some connection to family for so long it was instinctive, and exhausting.

But to pack up and leave, to give up all chance of running into her biological parents, or . . . give herself a chance to start fresh.

Sam had asked for her help. Offered her a place to start over by sharing his office space with her. Did she have the courage to make the move?

The driver's door opened. She realized something had banged in the truck bed while she mulled over her thoughts. Shivering, she wiggled against the leather seat to hide her unease.

"I've been thinking about what you said." She turned toward Sam as he fastened his seatbelt. Everything he'd said made sense. But . . . she couldn't take the chance. As long as he was around, she held on to the secret hope that he might notice her, grow to care for her. She was wasting time daydreaming about things that wouldn't happen.

"Good, I bought a pet carrier for Ben."

"Why?"

Sam shuddered under the attack of that one word. Uh-oh, he'd blown it now. "Did I mention the wraparound front porch?"

Ellie shook her head and kept her gaze on the passing scenery. Shivers ran over her as if a cloud had covered the sun. She loved a house with a porch.

"There's a room upstairs that would make the perfect place for you to sew while you make the curtains. And you can bring Ben with you."

Her head jerked toward him. "Are you mad? I can't stay at your house and make curtains. What about my shop?"

Sam parked on the street outside her newly cleaned door. The buildings on either side were vacant, with dirty windows that made the sparkle of hers look like a diamond in this deserted neighborhood.

"Couldn't you sew faster if you were close to the job?"

"Yes," she admitted as she unlocked the door and waited for him to walk past.

"You could bring Benny with you when you worked

at the house. He'd like the space." Sam glanced at the cat peering at them from sleepy eyes. The bribe bought him a stinging glance, so he rushed on with, "You'd be sure to pick up more customers."

Her chin tilted. Her lips thinned in that stubborn look he didn't trust. He could almost hear her refusing his offer.

He was out of ideas. If she didn't jump at this job offer, he had no way of making sure she had a safe place to stay. So, he played his last card. "It would help me, if you could see your way clear to doing this."

Guilt tasted bitter, Sam realized. He almost backed down, right then. He didn't like playing on her emotions. But he didn't have a choice. If she came to Redbud, he could watch over her, know she was safe. This had nothing to do with Shawn's dare. Sam shrugged off the twinge of guilt that nagged at his conscience as he watched her and waited. He should tell her about the dare.

Ellie's heart felt as if it were being wrenched from her chest. The expression in Sam's eyes made her want to follow him without asking any questions. What then? She had her sewing skills to depend on, nothing more. Letting her emotions sidetrack her could lead to disaster. As much as she wanted to help Sam—to be near him—it was better all around if she stayed here. Then she'd have to make a success of this business venture.

"Sam, I can't—"

A loud pounding rattled the front door. Ellie hurried toward the noise to see an older man glaring at her through the clean glass.

"Can I help you?" Her words dropped like ice pellets. It was all she could do to keep from pointing out the large greasy smudge his nose left on the clean glass.

Faded blue eyes glared at her from a face lined by years in the sun. Thinning hair matched the utility gray of the shirt that hung from his shoulders. She couldn't determine his age, but his skin looked as if he had shrunk.

"You Ellie—" he fumbled with the papers in his hand,"—Gray?"

"Yes?"

"I own this building." His eyes skittered past her to the fabric display in the window. If he had spied a dead rat instead of a rainbow of colorful fabric, his nose couldn't have turned up any more.

"Oh!" A deep breath shuddered through her. Her anger fizzled. "Nice to meet—"

"That sublease you signed with my former tenant ain't legal." His laser-like voice swiped through her tentative greeting, booming louder with each word. "The lease on this place runs out next week."

"Then I'd like to renew—"

"I want you out of here as soon as possible. Today would be good."

"But I—"

"I'm selling this building." His glare focused on the clean windows. "I sign the papers tomorrow."

Chapter Seven

"Will you come to Redbud now?" Sam hated the lost look that turned Ellie's eyes the color of swamp water. "You could make a new start in a new town." Life seemed to have drained out of her. "Redbud is small, but what we lack in amenities, we make up for in personality." His wheedling tone earned a reluctant grin, but the shadows didn't leave her eyes.

"Why? I can make your curtains without moving."

Sam concentrated on the toe of his boot, tracing the spots on the stained floor to hide his reaction. "What's holding you here?"

Ellie turned away, not wanting to admit the feelings gnawing at her insides. "It's all I know."

"Why not start over in a new place? Leave the past behind?"

"This is my home."

"Who would you call if you needed help?"

"Is that what this is about? You don't think I can take care of myself?" Ellie stepped so close to him that she stomped on the toe of his boot as she glared into his face. "I can take care of myself."

Sam met the angry sparkle in her glance, then darted a look around the room. Ellie's face flooded with color. He didn't have to say a word. Okay, this wasn't the best setup, but . . . what was holding her here?

"I know this town—"

"You'd like Redbud." His gut twisted. That was as close as he dared come to admitting he liked Ellie more than he felt was wise. "We have a great pizza place."

Ellie grinned, despite her heavy heart. Sam didn't know how hard he was to resist. But he knew she couldn't resist pizza. Still . . .

"What are you saying?" If he gave her the least bit of hope, she could . . . could what? Risk everything because she was attracted to him? "What does it matter? Why do you care?"

Sam looked like a steer cornered by a pack of wolves. Her heart sank. She'd phrased it all wrong. If he cared, whether she moved to Redbud or not, he wouldn't admit it now.

"Hey, don't make me sound so bossy!" Sam waggled his brows in that comical manner that usually made her grin. But she saw the tense look in his eyes. "I'm just trying to help. Redbud is a good place to live and there's that studio over the office that I told you about."

He sounded like a little kid rushing through his book report. Despite her disappointment that he hadn't made a personal comment, her spirits lifted. A weak laugh escaped. Being around Sam was good for her.

His startled reaction to the sound of her laugh turned to grin. "Overkill, huh?"

Ellie shook her head and grinned. "I'll give the situation some thought." She held up her hand when he opened his mouth. "But no matter what, I'll help you get ready for Shawn and Dawn's reception."

It was almost a relief to wave Sam off. Saying good-bye hurt less than she'd expected. Ellie blamed it on her disappointment that he didn't admit he had feelings for her, but she knew. Or maybe, after all this time, after being without a family for twenty-six years, she was hoping for more than he could give. Her attraction to Sam defied words. Did she dare act on instinct?

If she were honest, she would admit she had reached a decision. That's why it was easy to let him leave.

Maybe it was seeing Sam again. Maybe it was the feeling that what they shared was special. Or maybe it was getting booted out of this building.

Rejected by a landlord she hadn't met before today. Like so many other times, Ellie felt the sting of being turned away.

She was stronger now. She had faced rejection in the past . . . and survived. She was on her own. Didn't that make Sam's suggestion a sensible choice? She'd spent twenty-six years of her life in this town. All she had to show for it was a friendship with her former landlady and Benny.

Life was about choices. The old maids had drilled that in her head for years.

"You're leaving town, Ellie?" Miss Margaret's bright blue eyes searched Ellie's face. "I hate to see you go . . . but it could be the best thing for you."

Ellie gasped in surprise. She'd come to say goodbye to the only person she counted as a friend. But she hadn't expected this reaction. Her gaze on the wrinkled face, she said, "I'll miss you, Miss Margaret."

"I'll miss you too, child." A tiny hand patted her arm. "Emiline and Anastasia were proud of you, Ellie." The old lady smiled. "And so am I."

"Thank you, I—I hope they were." Tears filled her eyes. She didn't want Miss Margaret to see how moved she was by her words, but she couldn't run away. There was one last thing she had to know.

"Never doubt it, child. They didn't let on . . . they were too proud to let their feelings show. But they were my friends, and I know." Her blue eyes squinted as if she were looking back at the past. "You made their last years very happy."

Emotion clogged Ellie's throat. Twice in one day she had received confirmation she was valued as a person. It seemed strange. She'd been searching for approval all her life, and in one day she had the endorsement of two people she admired. "I appreciate you telling me that."

"Pshaw, child . . . if they hadn't been such old biddies, they'd have told you themselves."

Ellie started in surprise, then, seeing the humorous sparkle in eyes framed by wrinkles, she joined the old lady's laughter.

Shortness of breath stopped Miss Margaret. Ellie waited until the elderly woman stopped wheezing, then asked the question that burned in her brain.

"Miss Margaret . . . I've always wondered . . . did the sisters know who my parents were?"

"No, child, they didn't have a hint."

"Do you know?"

Warm affection filled the faded blue gaze. The tiny hand covered in age spots gripped Ellie's arm. "I wish I did, child, for your sake. I can't help you, except to say this: we were three old women who were as proud of you as if you belonged to us."

The minute she drove down Main Street, Ellie knew she had made the right choice. Redbud was like a small town in the movies.

Parking in front of a diner, in the shade of a big oak tree, Ellie heaved a sigh of mixed emotions. She was here. If she'd made the wrong choice, she'd try again. Armed with renewed courage from her talk with Miss Margaret, she was ready to start over.

From the looks of this town, she'd picked the right place, even without Sam's influence. She decided to grab a bite to eat before she faced him. Being around him made her insides feel hollow. Maybe food would help. After shaking cat food into Benny's bowl, she filled the water cup in his carrier, cracked open the windows, and left the car.

Inside, the diner looked like a picture out of an old magazine. Ceiling fans whirled, stirring air heavy with the aroma of onions, beef, and coffee. Large black and white tiles covered the floor. Red booths lined the walls. The center of the room was filled with tables and red-bottomed chairs. And along the side next to the kitchen, stools covered in red lined the counter.

Ellie loved the place on sight, just like the rest of the town. Sliding into an empty booth, she looked around, fascinated.

"What can I get you, hon?"

Ellie turned to the gum-smacking middle-aged blond batting mascara-laden lashes. Looking at the face wrinkled with time and humor, she grinned. "I'm new here. What do you recommend?"

"Cheeseburger, fries, and a Coke."

Making a tick on the tablet in her hand, the waitress twisted off like a pink whirlwind. In seconds, she was back, plopping a tinkling glass of ice and a soft drink can on the table with napkin-covered silverware. Then, darting a glance around the half-filled room, she slipped in the booth across from Ellie.

"Name's Stella. Tell me about yourself, hon."

Ellie grinned and took big sip of the cold drink,

wishing she had insisted on Pepsi. "My name's Ellie Gray." She set the glass down and returned Stella's inquisitive stare. "I didn't think small towns were friendly to newcomers."

Stella made a sound that could only be described as a cackle. "Some are, some aren't. Never seen a stranger, myself." Patting bleached-blond curls, she popped her gum again. "You in town visiting?"

"More like business. I'm thinking of opening a shop." She glanced around the room again. "Tell me about Redbud."

"Whatcha want to know? Who's sleeping with who? Or who's going to win a seat on the town board?" She laughed, a chicken-squawking sound Ellie realized was pure Stella.

Ellie grinned at the impish expression on her painted face. "How do you like living here?"

"Never left, buried two husbands, on the lookout for number four."

"Four? What happened to number—"

"Three? He's still kicking . . . but I like to be pre-pared." Stella cackled and stood up, looking over Ellie's shoulder to say, "How's it going, Sam?"

"Don't let her fool you. She's got that man hog-tied."

Delicious chills washed over Ellie. Her hand froze in the act of lifting her glass.

"Oh shush, Sam! You're giving away all my secrets." Stella's bright blue look darted from Ellie to the man taking the seat opposite her. "What'll ya have, Sam. Usual?"

"Yeah, thanks, Stell." Sam leaned his elbows on the edge of the table and smiled across at Ellie. "I saw the car. Figured I'd take a look, see if it was yours."

A grin pulled at her lips despite her effort to hide the quake going on inside her. "I decided to take a look at this place, since you recommended it so highly."

Sam grinned as he moved back for Stella to put his drink down. Eyebrows waggling, he said, "Eat up, I'll give you the tour."

Ellie waited for Stella to put down a plate loaded with a cheeseburger and fries.

"Share the fries, I'll bring more." She gave them a knowing glance and left them alone.

"She seems like fun."

Sam shrugged, reaching for a long strip of potato off her plate. "Are you here for good?"

Ellie's appetite disappeared. She had intended to look around before she met up with Sam. "Maybe." She stuffed a delicious strip of fried potato in her mouth and shrugged.

By the time they finished the meal, Stella had pried enough information out of Ellie to write a newspaper column.

"What about that space in your building, Sam?" Stella smacked gum as she refilled their soft drinks. "All those windows would give her good light to sew."

Ellie lifted a questioning brow, afraid to say a word.

"There's a one-room apartment upstairs, right?" Stella looked at Ellie. "You'll like it, hon."

Sam shoved to his feet. "We'll see you, Stella."

"Nice to meet you, Stella, the food was good." Ellie snatched her ticket from Sam's hand and trotted to the register.

"Stella has a way of running things." Sam unlocked the door to a building on the opposite side of the street.

Ellie tried to hide her excitement. Sam's office building occupied a corner a few doors down the street from the diner. The multi-paned glass door opened to a glass-enclosed foyer that led to a hall between two offices, both with glass walls down the length of the hall, giving little privacy but adding old world charm.

"I can't believe the walls are glass."

"This was built for a bank." Sam nodded toward the foyer. "The bank owner wanted to see his employees at all times . . . or so the story goes." He shrugged and looked around. "It's different."

Ellie stared at the polished hardwood floors. No dark oil stains here. Even the doors to each office were double doors. But it was the curved glass wall on the outside of the building that made her heart pitter-pat in her chest. *What a wonderful display window*, she thought as she followed Sam up a back staircase.

"This apartment is more of a loft, really."

Ellie sighed. After the place she'd left, the one-room studio looked glamorous. Still, she wasn't sure she wanted to be cooped up in the same building with Sam every day. "You mentioned there were other places available?"

Sam's frown wasn't what she'd expected.

She didn't mean to insult him, but—

"Yeah, in the next block. Come on, I'll show you."

"No! I mean . . . I was wondering how many vacancies there were in town." She didn't need a tour of the other buildings. "This building is perfect for me."

"Good. Let's get your things out of the car. We can take care of the legal matters after you get Benny settled."

Half an hour later, Ellie climbed the stairs with the last turn and stopped to rest against a worn sofa. "You don't mind if I have Benny here?"

"Nope!" Sam set the carrier down as he glanced at her. "We're pals, remember?"

"Right." Ellie grinned. Now wasn't the time to give Sam a lesson about independent cats. "This seems too good to be true."

"Come see my house."

Ellie drifted over to open cabinet doors in the one-wall kitchenette. "I want to sign the lease first."

Sam hid his disappointment and led the way downstairs. "You'll be safe here." He waved toward the glass. "The windows are real lead glass and reinforced. And the town cops patrol on a regular basis." He led the way to the double doors into the hall. "You'll have to register with the Chamber of Business, notify Town Hall, and attend Council meetings—"

"Sam—"

He settled behind a piled-up desk. "Business owners are expected to work on the chamber projects—"

"Sam—"

He shuffled through one drawer after another. "The

best way to fit in with the old-timers is to just let them have their say. They're a lot of hot air and bluff, but underneath, they're good-hearted. Though—"

"Sam!"

He looked at her with a frown. "What?"

"I can take care of myself!"

His frown deepened. He wanted to keep her from making mistakes. Failure was common with new business owners. Shucks, he'd been operating for years now, and he still feared losing his shirt. "I'm just trying to help."

Ellie spent a sleepless night. The bed was comfortable enough. And Benny settled down after a thorough inspection, with a full tummy, thanks to Sam's insistence that he take her to go get supplies.

Everything was organized . . . thanks to Sam.

That's what kept Ellie from sleeping. *Start like you mean to go* was one of the old maids' favorite sayings.

She had tried.

But Sam insisted on helping.

Maybe it was because she was in a new town. Or because she was sharing his office building?

Had it been a mistake to rent the shop from Sam? Even as she mulled over the questions, doubt filled her. Tomorrow she would see his house and check out the work he needed her to do. What if she wasn't up to the job?

Would coming to Redbud be the end of their friendship, despite her growing attraction to him?

* * *

When Sam walked in her shop early the next morning, every window sparkled. All her sewing supplies were stored away, and she had started sewing on a wedding dress.

The designer dress was nowhere in sight.

"Where's the gown?"

Ellie glanced up from the sewing machine, pretending she hadn't seen him coming. "Still packed," she said around a mouthful of pins. "I'm working on a gown to display in the window."

"Oh!" Sam held up a bag giving off a calorie-filled aroma. "Breakfast?" He frowned. "You shouldn't put pins in your mouth."

Her brow lifted as she sent him a glare. Seeing the sudden flush to his cheeks, she shook her head. Then, removing the pins, she said, "I ate hours ago, but thanks."

"Do you have time to go see my house?"

"Not really." Her tone dripped with reluctance. She didn't want visuals of Sam in his own home to add to the images that already danced through her head and kept her awake at night. Still, she owed him. She glanced up in time to see his frown.

"I'm working on some display samples. But I need to get started on your curtains too, so we'd better make time." She put the white satin fabric down carefully and stretched. "You need to fill me in on your plans."

Sam stopped the truck at the top of the drive. Ellie's breath caught with her first sight of the building. This wasn't just a house, she thought as a shudder traveled through her. This . . . this was what she'd missed, what she dreamed about for the future. Chill bumps popped out on her arms despite the heat of the August sun.

Now she understood why this property meant so much to Sam. A swift glance at his face as he looked around and everything fell into place. This was more than a building and acres of dirt; this property was a part of Sam, part of who he was. His strength, his determination, his kindness, all came from his connection to his past.

She sighed. It was up to her to help Sam, to make his house into a home—on the surface, at least. Tearing her gaze from his face, she forced her attention to her surroundings.

Protecting her heart just became more difficult.

Early rays of sun glanced off the many windows and the red metal roof. The large wraparound porch provided shelter from the hot summer sun. She imagined the porch filled with people, sitting around with glasses of iced tea, enjoying a leisurely visit. Chills raced along her arms all over again.

"It's so big."

"Yeah, too big . . ." After hearing the infliction in her voice Sam pulled his attention away from the house and glanced in her direction. The look on her face twisted his insides.

She knew! Ellie understood how he felt. But rather than soothing him, his sudden discovery sent panic slithering along his spine. He didn't need a woman sharing his feelings for this place.

Something inside him clicked. Fear grabbed him by

the back of the neck. He wasn't sure bringing Ellie here was a good idea after all. Despite his need to return this property to mint condition, he had mixed emotions. His mind might say he didn't need a woman to share his feelings for this house, but his heart didn't agree.

Everything about Ellie Gray set his plans on edge. He had endangered his need to finalize the deal with Shawn so he could keep Ellie safe.

Now her presence threatened all he loved by distracting him.

His life would be less complicated if he had just said goodbye and left her on her doorstep. But no, he had encouraged—make that all but insisted—that she come to Redbud. Come to the very property that Shawn had dared him to try to get for free by making Ellie fall for him.

Beads of sweat popped out on his forehead. Muscles in his neck and shoulders tightened. Sam glanced from the rapt look on Ellie's face to the house and felt the answering tug in his gut. Okay, so she understood his attachment to his home. Did that mean she had to get tangled up in his personal life?

So, why did you bring her here? Taunted by his conscience, he set the truck in motion. Okay, he was attracted to Ellie Gray. But he'd get over it.

"The heating bills are outrageous." He stared toward the house.

"I can imagine."

"That's one reason I wanted curtains up before cold weather." *And I want my house to look like a home.*

"Of course, now I need the house ready for Shawn's party."

Ellie's insides churned. Despite understanding Sam's situation, she wished she'd never laid eyes on this house. She couldn't shake the sudden feeling that her life would never be the same.

"It doesn't seem like his sort of place."

Sam sighed. "I wish I knew what he was up to."

Ellie darted a quick glance in his direction. Gone was the joy of showing her his house. His brow wrinkled. Her fingers itched to smooth his skin with a caress as she watched the sparkle disappear from his eyes. But she didn't dare. She bit down on her lower lip as her need to connect with Sam swamped her. This had to stop. Working with Sam was going to be hard enough without her emotions getting in the way.

He parked behind the house and pointed. "This sunroom was added when my grandfather was a child."

"It looks huge." Ellie stared at the floor-to-ceiling glass walls. She could imagine how it would look with the windows sparkling clean, large plants filling the space with lush greenery, and wicker furniture. She loved white wicker furniture.

"It needs a lot of work."

"I'd better get Ben out of his cage." She gulped air and reached for the pet carrier. "Are you sure you don't mind having him in the house?"

"I'm sure." He pushed her hand away and lifted the carrier. He had never had a pet. He hadn't realized that until he watched Ellie hold the big cat in her arms for the first time. All his life, he'd been surrounded by family. His childhood should have been different from Ellie's.

But even though he had lived with his grandparents, the love that should have surrounded him had been lacking. His grandfather had been twisted with regret over losing his home.

His grandmother had been tormented by what his grandfather's regrets had done to him. She had wasted away, filled with remorse because she couldn't make her husband happy.

He had grown up in surroundings almost as sterile as he guessed Ellie's past had been, but she had animals to love. He hadn't. That's one of the reasons he had suggested she bring the cat.

"I'm looking forward to having another male around the house." Sam arched a brow in her direction. "This house is going to be ruled by males."

"Right!" Ellie laughed as she followed him through the back door. "I hate to disappoint you, being outnumbered by males and all, but I think you're in for a shock."

Sam put the cage on the counter. Working at the latch to open the door, he spoke over the noise from the complaining animal. "What do you mean?"

"Well." Ellie pushed his hand aside before he could reach into the cage. Now was not the time for Sam to learn Benny had his own ideas of where his loyalty belonged. "Ben might be male, but that doesn't count with him."

"What are you saying?" Amusement filled Sam's eyes as he watched her ease the big tom out of his prison. "He doesn't like being a boy?"

Ellie hugged the harassed cat to her chest for a quick squeeze and then put him on the floor. "As far as Ben is concerned, he rules. People are inferior."

Their laughter filled the room as Ben sniffed around the kitchen. Ellie noticed that despite the large windows, the room was dark. "Are you changing anything in here?"

"I've had all the wiring replaced and updated the heat. Feel the cool air?" Crossing to a door that led to the hall, he motioned for her to follow. "Now it's time to slap on some paint. New appliances are at the bottom of my list. Come see the rest of the place while Ben makes himself at home."

By the time they finished measuring the windows, Ellie was tired. The upheaval of moving and a sleepless night were catching up with her.

"I'm bushed," she said, glancing at her watch. "It's after five. We've put in a full day."

"I'm thinking the same thing. Are you hungry?" Sam opened the refrigerator. "Whoa, that was a mistake." He slammed the door and grabbed her arm. "Let's go get a pizza."

Ellie spotted the laden basket of goodies as she opened the door of the shop after a quick stop for pizza. Sam's bookkeeper must have let the delivery person in. Ripping into the small envelope, she read, "Welcome to Redbud. Town Council Meeting tonight, at seven, attendance required for all newcomers." She waved the card at Sam.

"I should have warned you. We got busy and I forgot about the meeting tonight."

"It's six-thirty now. Where is the meeting?"

"At the Town Hall." Sam frowned. "Look, some of the old-timers aren't very friendly at first. Just don't pay them any attention."

"Second order of business is what to do with all the strays around town." The chairman's raspy voice grated on the pain behind Ellie's eyes.

What strays? Did he mean her? Ellie stifled a tired giggle and tried to focus. Meeting the new members had been the first order of business. She felt as if she'd been x-rayed by the grim expressions, flogged by questions, abused by suspicious looks, and just plain rejected.

Small towns were cliquish. She expected to be on the fringe of things for a while. Sam had warned her. And she was still feeling the pain of rejection from her last attempt at being a business tenant. Tonight's reception didn't sit well.

Sam suggested she play wallflower for a meeting or two. Wait until the chairman called her to do something, and then make her place in the group. It was good advice, but she had tried to curb her frustration as one comment after the other distracted attention from the order of business. The old maids always warned her to think first and act later, but she didn't like wasting time—or feeling invisible.

It irked her that Sam seemed to find her so since she'd arrived in town. Okay, it had only been twenty-four hours. What had she expected? A welcome kiss?

Ummm . . . not a bad idea. Maybe if she were a little more secure with his welcome, she wouldn't think twice about being accepted by a bunch of strangers. Why should she let Sam's lack of encouragement bother her? They had worked side by side all day. They worked well together, she thought. Of course, she would, considering every minute she spent with Sam was like a trip to the candy store.

She had worked for her independence for the past ten years. That's why, after long minutes of rambling comments that offered no solution, she opened her mouth.

"Sponsor a spay and neuter clinic."

"How are we going to pay for that, missy?"

Twenty sets of eyes turned to stare at her. There would have been more, but Sam and his friend Stan were on a committee that had left the room for a special session. The issue of growing population of pets had been tossed back and forth for ten minutes without any suggestions.

Now Ellie wished she'd kept her mouth shut. Almost. The truth was, she was tired of worrying about rejection. This time, she had chosen the place she wanted to live. She was going to make a spot for herself.

"Have a block-long bake sale."

"What do you mean by block-long bake sale?"

Ellie faced the wrinkled man with a smile. "Have enough tables and booths to stretch a block."

"She's right! Almost everyone has a sweet tooth."

"But who would come?"

"I can bake my special brownies," said a woman wearing a brown sweater.

Ellie smiled at her. The brown sweater belonged to the librarian, she thought. At least she had some support. Then she opened her mouth again. "You need to plan some event to draw a crowd!" It was a good thing Sam was out of the room.

"Like what?"

"We don't have that many people in town."

"Who would come when they can bake at home?"

Ellie sighed. Sam wouldn't like this one bit. She hadn't intended on getting involved. She'd just made a suggestion. "You need something like a skills auction to attract a crowd."

The noise over that discussion almost brought the roof down. Sam stuck his head in the door and met her glance with a raised brow.

Ellie shrugged and grinned.

Satisfied that she looked okay, Sam turned away. Thirty minutes later, both suggestions were passed by a large majority.

"Third order of business," the chairman announced. Ellie had learned his name was Miller. "Old man Jenson's cabbage patch has the neighbors in an uproar."

Ellie tried not to laugh at the details of excess produce wasting away in the garden. Glancing around, she waited for the obvious, but no suggestions were made. Thinking of all the time she was wasting, Ellie did what she'd promised she wouldn't do again tonight. "Sponsor a farmer's market. Attract traffic to the downtown area."

Amid the hubbub that followed, Sam's committee returned to the room. Just as he was seated, Mr. Miller called for a vote on the farmer's market idea.

Ellie grinned at Sam, shrugged at his look of confusion, and quickly raised her hand.

"Passed by majority," Mr. Miller called out. "Now how long will it take to organize?"

"Produce is in season now," a gruff voice said. Ellie thought it was the barber.

"Put a notice in the paper. Every business in town could pass out flyers and spread the word." Ellie clamped her mouth shut as she met Sam's startled glance.

"Bakery might object to the bake sale."

"It will take some business, but the increased foot traffic should help sales. I run the bakery, I vote yes."

Laughter filled the room to cheers of "Good ole Adge."

Sam frowned, clearly not understanding what he'd missed. Ellie met his questioning look with a shrug and grinned. He'd find out soon enough.

"Where will we get that many tables?"

"We'll need permits."

"Have to clear it with the police chief."

"Sam, can you talk to the chief about blocking off the street for the farmer's market?" Chairman Miller demanded.

Sam sent Ellie a glance loaded with questions as he answered, "Sure."

When the meeting broke up, Sam's expression registered surprise when most of the members came by to shake Ellie's hand and welcome her to the meeting.

"What did you do while I was out?" he demanded as they walked the block to his office.

"I just made a suggestion or two."

"Like what?"

"Oh, they need money to spay and neuter the strays, so . . . I suggested a block-long bake sale."

"You what?"

Ellie grinned under cover of darkness. Even with the streetlights on, it wasn't that bright. Maybe she should suggest to the council that they improve the lighting. Turning, she saw his frown. Or, maybe she would keep her mouth shut for a while.

"Well—"

"I thought you were going to play it safe till they got to know you."

The pounding behind her right eye got heavier. Heat rushed to her face. "What's wrong, Sam? Don't you think women have brains?"

Air whooshed out of his lungs loud enough for Ellie to hear over the clicking of their steps on the sidewalk.

"That's not the issue and you know it." He glared in the semi-darkness.

"I'm sorry. That wasn't fair."

"I just . . ." Sam's voice dwindled off.

Seconds passed. The corner building was in sight. "What, Sam?"

Regret filled his tone. "I didn't want you to get a cold shoulder, okay?"

Ellie's anger evaporated completely. "Oh, Sam!" She lunged against his chest and pulled his cheek down for a kiss.

All was well, perfect even. With her chest flattened against his, Ellie could hear the rush of his heart racing in time with her own.

Then, as she started to ease away, everything changed.

Sam put his arms around her, held her close, and angled his head so his lips covered hers.

Chapter Eight

Do you know what it's like to want something so bad you'd do anything to get it?

Ellie pushed fabric through the sewing machine while her words—and the memory of Sam's kiss—taunted her.

She glanced at the clock. She had been sewing since five, even before the sun came up. The wedding dress was finished.

Taking a moment to stretch, she admired the floating white gown on display in the window and sighed. On one hand, she'd never been happier.

The wedding dress had gone together like a dream, even with the off-the-shoulder puffs and the sweetheart neckline. She had used skills she had learned from Sae Wong. The finished dress showed the improvement in her sewing.

But. . . . She glanced across the hall as she heard a

noise. Marge Corbin, the bookkeeper, waved. Ellie's disappointment was all the proof she needed that all wasn't well in her new world.

After Sam had left her at the door last night, she had sewed on the wedding gown for a couple of hours before going to bed. Between tossing and turning, she dreamed of being held close in his arms, of feeling safe.

Releasing a deep sigh, she turned back to work and pressed her foot to the pedal. Fabric flew through the machine. It was a good thing she was only making strips for a quilt. If she had abused the fragile fabric of the wedding gown this way, the dress would be in shreds. She needed to let off steam.

Oh, yes, she knew what it was like to want something so bad you'd do anything to get it. She was in Redbud, wasn't she? She knew what it felt like only too well, and that's what scared her.

Starting over in a new town made good sense. For the first time in her life she could greet people on the street and not wonder if she was speaking to her own parents. That was a relief. And she liked Redbud. The more people she met, the better she liked the area.

Her emotions were out of control, she admitted as she backstitched the seam. Grabbing two more pieces of fabric, she started to sew while her mental lecture continued. She was falling for Sam Oglethorpe. Not that she'd ever been in love before, but she knew the signs. Sweaty palms, racing heart, the need to see him constantly. All were signs that she was in big trouble.

She glanced across the hall again, but only Marge's face showed through the glass wall. Sam didn't share her feelings . . . at least, she didn't think he did. Men were different. They hugged and kissed a woman because she was a woman, right?

Well, Ellie Gray didn't kiss just any man. When Sam had pulled her close and kissed her last night, her world toppled. Her hand touched her lips again. The heat from Sam's kiss still made her lips twitch . . . her heart race . . . her palms sweat.

She gave the fabric an impatient toss and stood up. The sewing machine could use a break. She needed to move, to do something. She had the long room divided into work and display areas by arranging the storage bins left by the previous tenant. Now she searched for something to do.

Work would take her mind off Sam. Off his kiss. Off the way his embrace made her feel safe. That's what scared her.

Who was she kidding? Sam was one of the nicest men she had ever met. Falling for him would be so easy. That's why she was determined to prove that she was immune to his charm. She needed to prove she could take care of herself.

Now if he would just come to work, so she could put her plan in action. And then he appeared. Looking through the glass, Ellie saw him sitting at his desk, talking on the phone. Sometime in the last five minutes, while she battled with her conscience, he had arrived without her notice.

Maybe she wasn't falling for him after all. Wouldn't her personal radar know when he was near, if she were in that deep? Either way, she had business to talk over with him. The sooner she faced him, the better she would feel.

She knocked on the open door. "Morning, Marge. Sam available?"

"Hey, Ellie, he's on the phone. Did you find your gift basket last night?"

"Yes, thanks." Ellie grinned at the middle-aged woman. "I had some of those delicious pastries from the bakery for breakfast."

"They're great." Marge held up a bag similar to the one Ellie had pulled her own pastries out of earlier. "The bakery opens around five, in case you get hungry for cinnamon rolls."

"I can't eat many of those with all the sitting—"

"Eat what?"

Her heart pounding in her throat, Ellie turned toward Sam. "Pastries."

"Ellie has discovered the bakery's secret."

Sam grinned. "I guess you don't want breakfast at the diner, then?"

Ellie swallowed the lump in her throat and shook her head. "I do need a minute of your time, though." It was hard trying to appear normal when her arms ached to wrap around his neck. "Do you have a minute?"

"Sure, walk with me." His hazel eyes danced with humor. Ellie was sure she had pudding on her face or had left a button undone. However, her quick check as she followed him across the street proved nothing was amiss.

"You look good this morning."

His voice, low and gravelly, plucked at her nerves. Her stomach threatened to turn upside down. A warm flush rushed to her cheeks. Just at the point of melt-down, her pride surged to life. She could not let Sam see how he affected her. She just couldn't. Tilting her chin, eyeing his broad shoulders covered by a navy T-shirt, she winked up at him as she stepped through the door he held and into the aromatic heat of the diner.

"Thanks, you don't look so bad yourself."

Stella whirled past and called, "Take a seat."

Ellie dropped into the first empty booth before her knees folded. Sam slid in the opposite side and grinned. That did it. Her heart started pounding like the wings of a hummingbird. She had to stop this. "Umm, I have some questions—"

Stella plunked down two cups of coffee. "What'll you have, hon?"

"Just coffee, thanks. How are you, Stella?"

"Same ole, same ole."

"What's got you so riled, Stella?" Sam reached for a steaming cup.

Popping her gum, Stella pulled cream and sugar to the center of the table. "Aw, ole Pete Ritter's complaining about the bake sale, no offense, hon." She reached to pat Ellie's hand. "You know how folks are, but it really fries my taters that some people never want to try anything new." She glanced around the roomful of customers. "What for ya, Sam, the usual?"

"Yeah . . . oh, and bring Ellie that Mexican omelet special of Roy's, okay?" Sam grinned at Ellie's start of surprise. "You can't sew all day on pastry."

"Sam! I can take care of myself."

"Sorry, just trying to be sociable."

"Well, back off. I'm not your sister!"

"Honey." Voice low, Sam leaned across the table. His eyes, glinting with green sparks, raked over her face, one feature at a time. In a voice as slow as warm molasses, he said, "Honey, believe me, I know you are not my sister." His glance rested on her mouth for long, long seconds before he settled back against the seat.

Ellie came out of her daze and realized she had been leaning across the table toward him. Slumping against the back of the seat, she struggled to breathe. This was not good. The noise of dishes clinking and people talking finally registered in her head.

"Sorry," she mumbled, dropping her gaze to her cup. "I just—"

"Here ya go!" Stella plopped down plates and topped up the coffees in a quick motion. "Eat up."

Sam's mouth opened as if he were about to say something, but he shrugged and gave her a grin. "Let's eat, I'm starved. Hey, I saw the dress in the window. It looks great."

Ellie's tension escaped like air from a balloon. Sam's grin reassured her. As he tackled his food, her muscles relaxed. Maybe it was best to ignore the last few minutes. Watching his breakfast disappear, she grinned. She could do this. She could be friends with Sam, even if it broke her heart. At least she'd be doing the sensible thing.

"I finished it this morning." She took a deep breath. "Sam, I—"

"How's the loft? You adjusting to the new place?"

"Yes, I—"

"Like the omelet? Roy makes the best around."

Ellie tasted the fluffy mixture on her plate and sighed. "It's great, but I—"

"We don't have a Mexican restaurant around here, so Roy experiments with a couple of recipes. You should try his spicy wings sometime."

Ellie sighed. This wasn't like Sam, talking nonstop. Then it hit her. He was nervous. Was he thinking about the kisses they shared last night? What else? "Sam, I—"

Sam raised his head to peer around the room. "Where's Stella? It's not like her to let my cup get dry."

Ellie noticed the muscles bunched along his jaw and tried not to grin. Okay, so the big strong man was as uneasy as she was.

"I need to talk to you about the job." Sam's shoulders dropped a couple of inches at the mention of work. What was he worried about? Did he think she'd bring up that kiss? And make a spectacle of herself by melting at his feet? No way.

"Thanks, Stella, great coffee."

"I can't start work on the curtains until you give me some ideas."

Sam drained his cup. "I can't stop now, I'm running late. How about tonight? At the house? I'll cook."

"No, I'll cook, you bought pizza last night."

"Okay, you cook. And we'll talk. I'll pick you up after work." He grabbed the ticket and charged toward the front.

Ellie watched his broad back until he was out of sight, and sighed. He sure was jumpy. She started to get up, but noticed she had barely touched the omelet.

Maybe she would finish it before she left. She settled back in the booth. She didn't want to run into Sam again this morning.

Sam sighed as he pushed back from the table. Spaghetti was one of his favorite foods. Wouldn't you know Ellie made the best he'd ever eaten? The fact that she was a good cook just added to his problems.

He was having second thoughts about talking Ellie into moving to Redbud. Having her around made him forget his goal, made him want things he couldn't have until he settled the land deal.

"Let me get that." He reached for the serving dish. "How did you learn to cook like this?"

"Miss Emiline and Miss Anastasia made sure I earned my keep." Ellie grinned and turned toward the sink.

"So they taught you to cook?"

"Uh-huh." Ellie dipped a large pot in the dishwater. "Well, between their instructions and what I learned from my home economics teacher."

"Aha, that explains it." Sam took the soapy pot from her hands, rinsed it under the hot water, and started drying. He enjoyed joking with Ellie. It was relaxing after a busy day. He had let things go on too long. It was time to get down to business.

He intended to put a new plan into action tonight. He wasn't proud of it, but they would both be better off, in his opinion. "Ellie, we need to talk."

"Good. I was hoping you'd have time to go over my notes. You don't work on Saturday, do you?"

Sam swallowed past the lump threatening to choke

him. He hadn't expected her to help him broach the subject of her leaving.

"No." His voice sounded like a foghorn. Okay, so he admitted he liked having her around. She made him laugh. She cooked like a dream. But he hadn't bargained on her invading his thoughts night and day. He had asked her to make curtains for his house.

All he'd intended was to give her a job. "I keep weekends free so I can work on the house."

Ten minutes later, he slouched on the overstuffed floral sofa from his grandmother's living room and watched Ellie. She sat in a matching chair facing the sofa, her brow wrinkled. She looked cute as she flipped through a notebook she clenched like a life raft. He was relieved that she had finished measuring most of the windows. That made his new scheme easier to carry out.

"Where do you want to start?" He wanted to get this conversation over. Maybe tomorrow he could get some work done around this place.

His breath caught as she scribbled on the paper in her hand and tapped her toe on the floor. He could hear the pencil scratching against the tablet. When she looked at him across the coffee table, he noticed her eyes were a dull green.

He would miss seeing her if she left, but that was the problem. He couldn't get involved with her. Kissing her took his mind off his goal.

"That's the problem, Sam." She waved the notepad in the air. "I don't know where to start." She flipped through several sheets of paper. "I don't even know what colors you like."

"Is that all?" He didn't like the weak feeling in his stomach. Stronger men than he had been brought to their knees by a woman. His hand trembled as he lifted the tea glass to his mouth. Ellie's voice vibrated with tension and something else he couldn't identify. "What does it matter?"

"See!" she accused, sending him a glare. Then she jumped to her feet and stalked across the room. "Look at this!" She pointed to the floral sofa. "And this." Her finger jabbed toward the dark brown chair that had belonged to his grandfather. The sight of the frayed fabric twisted Sam's gut. "Look at these windows, Sam."

Sam forced his glance away from the splendid view of her rigid figure and glanced at the four large windows in the room. He'd much rather study her tall, slender silhouette. With that wild look in her eyes, he had better do as she asked.

"So?" It was an unusual arrangement to have windows beside the fireplace. He didn't see the problem. "Okay, so the windows were bunched on one end of the room. What was wrong with that? I like the windows."

"The windows aren't the problem," she snapped.

"Then I don't know what you mean. What is the problem?" If she was this frustrated over one room, maybe she was trying to tell him she didn't want the job after all. "Don't you want the job?" He tried to stifle the hopeful tone that tinted his words.

"It's not that."

"Oh?" His heart dropped to the toe of his boots.

"Of course I want the job." She twirled around in a

circle. "I love this house." She darted to the back of the couch, forcing him to glance over his right shoulder as a new fear took root in his gut. "I just don't know what you want, Sam."

I want you to leave. I want my space. I want my life back. I want to be able to sleep at night without thinking about you. Sam cleared his throat and croaked, "What do you mean?"

"There's a lot of work to be done here."

His heart leaped. Was she serious? "I know that."

"I need your help."

"Wait a minute." Sam surged to his feet and whirled to face her. "I hired you because I need this place presentable for Shawn's party."

He stalked over to lean on the mantle over the fireplace. This was working out better than he'd planned. A few more minutes of this and she would quit. He would be left in a bind trying to get the house ready for Shawn and Dawn's visit, but he'd manage.

With a little luck, he would never have to admit that Ellie controlled his dreams.

"I understand you're busy with work." Her low voice startled him as she placed her warm hand on his arm. "Don't worry!"

A surge stronger than any static electricity he'd ever felt sizzled along the hair on his arm. When had she crossed the room? He hadn't heard her approach as he'd braced himself on the mantel and stared into the empty fireplace. But he felt the charge of her touch.

The least little pressure from her pink nails and he was ready to jump out of his skin. Oh, yeah, this was going good, all right. His nerves were jumping like half-cooked frog legs. Lifting his gaze from her hand, he looked into her bottle-green eyes. Uh-oh! Mistake. His insides twisted.

"Don't worry?" That's all he could squeeze past the band tightening around his chest.

"I need to know how you picture the rooms looking, not your physical labor."

Relief washed over Sam. Inhaling deeply, he started to breathe. Okay, so she wasn't asking him to spend more time with her. Why didn't he feel relieved? He didn't want her in his life, did he?

His glance landed on the big cat sitting in his grandfather's chair. "Do you hear that, Ben? She needs my brain." He moved to scratch the cat's head, anything to hide his reaction to Ellie's touch. Oh, man! He had plenty of ideas. He could tell Miss Ellie Gray exactly what he wanted. And it had nothing to do with her leaving. Sam willed his hand steady as he rubbed the cat. "Quite a switch, don't you think, ole boy?"

The sound of Ellie's tinkling laugh joined his hard-sought chuckle. He moved back to slump on the sofa. This wasn't going well at all.

Ellie watched Sam's uneven step toward the sofa and wondered about his unusual clumsiness as she collapsed in the chair behind her.

What was going on? One minute they were getting along fine. The next thing she knew, the tension was thick enough to serve with whipped cream. She knew what was bothering her, but what was Sam's problem?

Sneaking a quick peep at his expression, she leaned

over to pick up the notebook. She could still feel the tingling heat of his skin. Touching him had been a mistake. How was she to know her innocent touch would bring her hand in contact with a forearm that bulged with muscle and felt like a powerful machine?

The heat from his skin, along with the power radiating off his body, turned her insides to mush. Ellie struggled to keep from trembling. One thing she knew for sure: her mind and body reacted to Sam's touch. That wasn't good, not if she wanted to keep her feelings from him.

Clearing her throat, she said, "I need to know what's on your mind."

Sam choked on a piece of ice. This was it. All he had to do was open his mouth and—

"I mean, do you want paint on the walls, or wallpaper? What are your favorite colors?" She glanced up from her notes. "Things like that."

Sam's jaw worked but no sound came out. Did he hear a slight tremble in her voice? He suspected his voice would shake, if he could find his tongue.

"Men don't think about things like that, I know. But I have to be honest with you."

Sam's chest tightened as his brain filled with new hope. Maybe she was just working up to the point. Maybe she would say the job was more than she wanted to tackle, that she wanted to leave. That's what he wanted, right?

"Curtains are usually the last thing added to a room."

"Really?" Okay, here it comes. He heard the frustration in her voice. "What are you saying?"

"I'm not an expert, you know." Ellie grinned as her glance met his. "But I think we got ahead of ourselves on this job."

You said that right, honey. Sam's heart pounded in his chest. She was going to suggest he hire someone else. Sounded like a good idea to him. Just having her around for a few hours made him edgy. He could get used to coming home to Ellie's quirky smile. And that put him in danger. "What do you mean?"

"Welll." Her voice trailed off as she glanced around.

Sam held his breath and silently begged her to just spit it out. Tell him she wanted to quit. Get it over with. Let it be her suggestion, so he wouldn't feel like a weasel wiggling out of their deal.

"I think you need to decide what you want to do with each room first."

So far, so good. Half a dozen more words and she would tell him she was out of there. "Oh?"

"We should go over each room, and you can decide what you want with colors, wallpaper, things like that, and I'll take notes."

"Sounds like a plan." Sam waited for her to say the magic words, but she didn't mention quitting.

"This house needs a lot of work." Ellie turned her hundred-watt smile on him. "But I could start on the curtains if I have some idea of what you wanted."

What he wanted? He wanted her to leave. He wanted to get his mind back on his goal. His mouth opened. "Would you take on the whole job? Nothing drastic, just paint and curtains." *Dadgumit. Where had that come from?* She'd been on the verge of quitting . . .

hadn't she? Then he opened his mouth and asked her to do more work. To invade his space even more. What was he thinking? "I'll help with the painting."

Ellie wasn't sure which of them was more surprised. Taking on a job that meant spending more time with Sam wasn't the smartest thing she could do right now.

"You'll have to help . . . if I agree to do the work, I mean." She looked around the room while her heart danced a jig in her chest. "I'll be busy with the curtains and getting ready for the bake sale."

"Why did you volunteer to organize that, anyway?" Sam paced around the sofa. The impatient tone of his voice had nothing to do with the bake sale and everything to do with putting his foot in his mouth. Now Ellie would be around more than before. "I thought you were going to let them get to know you, before you—"

"They were wasting time hashing over things that didn't matter—"

"Welcome to town politics." Sam glared from behind the sofa. He stood with his hands on his hips, revealing his impatience. But was it with the council's decision-making, or with her?

"Okay, so I didn't take your advice," she snapped. This wasn't how she wanted things to go with Sam. "But you live here. You don't understand—"

"Could be that I do."

Ellie clutched the notebook to her chest and met his dark gaze, feeling the heat of his look all the way to her toes. "What do you mean?"

"Could it be that you wanted to be accepted into the group, not pushed to the sidelines like a useless visitor?"

"Sam—"

"So you volunteered to bust your buns getting a bake sale and farmer's market organized."

"Well—"

"You were already in a bind trying to get your shop open and make curtains before the party."

"What's wrong, Sam?" Ellie jumped to her feet and glared across the room. "Afraid I'll make a mess of things and embarrass you? Or . . . or do it right, and prove you wrong?"

"What?"

His start of surprise relieved Ellie's tension. With his mouth open, his eyes glittering, and his brows arched at an alarming angle, he looked like a character out of a comedy. When his jaw started working but nothing left his mouth, she lost control.

Giggles filled the room. Sam blinked. Ellie's shoulders shook, her eyes glowed, and . . . yep . . . she was laughing. Shaking his head, his breath expelled a sigh as a reluctant grin pulled at his mouth. He would never understand women. One minute Ellie looked mad enough to chew nails; the next, she was laughing.

"Let's get to work," she gasped between giggles.

That was one of the things he loved about Ellie. She never took herself too seriously.

Whoa . . . stop! His humor took a plunge. Okay, he liked it when Ellie laughed, but love? That was off-limits, forbidden territory.

Pulling on his last resource, he managed a grin. "Okay, you're the boss." As his words echoed in the room, he shuddered. Fear, the kind known to every bachelor, filled his gut. Impatience flowed through him, causing his jerky movement toward the door and showing in his tone of voice. "Keep everything downstairs white."

"All white?"

"White or beige, then."

"You don't want to experiment—"

"I don't have time to experiment," Sam snapped, then noted the hurt look on her face and forced himself to relax. "Those flimsy-looking curtains—"

"Sheers?"

"Yeah, sheers, I can add color later, if I change my mind."

Ellie shrugged. "That's safe enough."

"But you can paint some of the rooms upstairs Carolina blue."

Ellie's expression cleared. "Blue—"

"Carolina blue."

". . . is always good."

"With white trim, and white curtains."

"You're sure?" Ellie followed him up the stairs.

Chapter Nine

Sam didn't want her to goof up, she knew that, Ellie admitted as her fingers guided the fabric through the sewing machine. But what else did he want? Why was he so uptight about her participation in the town council meeting?

Backstitching the end of the seam, she snipped off the loose threads and picked up another panel. In the two days since her tour of Sam's house, she'd finished half of the dining room curtains.

Lucky for her, Nell's department store down the block carried the fabric for sheers in their fabric department. She was thrilled to have a source of fabric on the next corner. It seemed like a good sign. Still . . .

The bell over the door tinkled. Excitement sizzled through her, but she forced herself to keep her attention on the sewing machine until she reached the end of the seam. She hadn't seen Sam since Friday night, but she didn't want to seem eager.

"Hello?"

Ellie looked up to see a middle-aged woman examining the bridal gown. Her heart dropped. Okay, so it wasn't Sam. But this was her first customer!

"May I help you?" Ellie lifted the armful of curtain fabric off her lap as she stood.

"Someone did a lovely job on this wedding dress."

Ellie's smile warmed to a genuine welcome. "I made the dress." She held out her hand. "I'm Ellie Gray. Welcome to my shop."

"I wasn't sure you were really open for business."

Ellie pretended not to hear the loaded question. What did this woman mean? "I don't have many samples ready for display—"

"You really can sew?"

Color rushed to Ellie's face as she met the woman's intent stare. "I love to sew. Is there something I can do for you?"

"I was just checking." Hard eyes examined Ellie from head to toe. "You could be stashed here because you're Sam's girlfriend."

Ellie's heart jumped to her throat. Had someone heard about the fake wedding? Sam would hate that. He wanted to start his future without the shadow of gossip.

The implication wasn't flattering to Ellie, either. That's when her pride came to the rescue and loosened her tongue.

"Ma'am, I can assure you I am a competent seamstress." Ellie lifted her chin as she returned the woman's x-ray stare. "I haven't known Sam long enough to form anything but a business relationship. Now, if I can't be of service, you'll have to excuse me. I'm busy."

Ellie started to move, but the woman blocked her way. The gray head bobbed and the blue floral dress swirled as the woman made a quick move to stick out her hand. "Pauline Morgan." Intent blue eyes studied Ellie as she said, "The mayor's wife. You'll get used to blunt speaking, if you're here long enough."

Ellie turned to rearrange a pillow display, trying to hide her amusement. Evidently she was supposed to be impressed with Mrs. Morgan's status. But she was in town to establish a new life. "Does that mean I call you Mrs. Mayor?"

Loud laughter filled the room. "Law, child!" Humor filled the bright blue eyes. "There's some in town that would say so, but you can call me Pauline."

Ellie grinned, liking the woman despite their rocky start. At least she'd been warned. Now she knew her presence in town was a topic of conversation. "Well, Pauline, what can I do for you?" Even though she was rushed with Sam's curtains, she needed more customers.

"I'm the welcoming committee." Pauline picked up one of the decorative pillows. "We're glad you settled in Redbud." She laid the pillow down and drifted over to a stack of miniature quilts. "Did you make these?"

"Yes," Ellie said and smiled. The sisters had insisted that she learn to quilt. But her love for the art focused more on miniature reproductions than on full-sized quilts. "Do you quilt?"

Pauline nodded, still looking at the tiny quilts in her hands. "We used to have a quilting bee. Too bad we let it slide. You do good work."

"Thank you!" Ellie beamed. "Are there many quilters around?"

"Half a dozen or so," the older lady said as she moved to the full-sized quilt Ellie had folded over a chair.

"That seems like enough."

Pauline looked over her shoulder with a bright stare. "Enough for what?"

"To start a quilting bee."

Pauline threw her head back and laughed. "Girl, you already have your hands full, from what I hear."

Ellie's brow wrinkled. "What do you mean?"

Pauline chuckled. "You set the town council on its ear the other night with that bake sale idea. And from what I heard at church yesterday, you're making curtains for that big house of Sam's."

"Well, yes—"

"When are you planning on starting up a quilting bee?"

Ellie took a deep breath, ready to prove she could. Then caution—and maybe a little of the old sisters' wisdom—took over. "Maybe you could help me?"

Surprise and then amusement covered Pauline's features as she reached to pat Ellie's arm. "I will, girl, I will." She turned toward the door. "I have a couple of dresses I need hemmed. I'll be back."

From that moment on, visitors were constant until after three that afternoon. Lillian from the dime store needed new curtains for her kitchen. Evie from the Snip 'n' Curl wanted Ellie to take two uniform jackets and make a long one. Sophie from the antique store needed a new suit hemmed. And so it went, one customer after the other, until Ellie had a list of ten or more jobs coming in.

Exhausted and thrilled, she managed a couple of hours' work on the curtains before she locked the doors at five.

"Hi, Marge!" Ellie lunged through the door across the hall. Sam's bookkeeper worked two or three days a week, depending on the workload. Ellie wanted to catch her before she left for the day.

"You've had a busy day." Marge looked up from straightening her desk.

Ellie slumped in the chair facing Marge and propped herself on its arm. "It's been crazy." She grinned. "Mostly curiosity, I think, but they all promised to bring work. Well, Evie from the beauty shop brought her uniforms with her."

"You'll get used to the snooping. It's part of living in a place where everyone knows your name."

Ellie shrugged. "I kinda like it . . . so far, but I wanted to get over here before you left." She waved the sheet of paper clutched in her left hand. "Where can I get signs for the bake sale copied?"

"Let me see." Marge reached for the paper, then frowned. "You need to make this on the computer before you copy it."

"I guess it would look better—"

"And get more interest. Give me a minute." In no

time, Marge picked a sheet out of the printer and passed a neat sign with a picture of baked goods to Ellie. "Run this over to the town hall. Emma Proctor, the mayor's secretary, works from noon until—"

"Proctor? The police chief's wife?"

"Very good! You're recognizing names."

"What names?"

Heart thumping in her chest, Ellie turned. "Hey, Sam! I've have to get to town hall. Thanks, Marge!" She rushed for the door, all exhaustion erased from her mind. One glimpse of Sam's face did that to her. This was silly. She was as lightheaded as if she'd been running. Sam was just a man, for crying out loud. But . . . what a man . . .

"Wait up, Ellie." Sam turned to Marge. "I need to see the chief about permits for the farmers' market. See you tomorrow."

Catching up with Ellie on the sidewalk, he said, "You had a good day?"

Ellie slowed her charge across Main Street and glanced up, noticing his tired expression. Someone else had spent sleepless nights, from the looks of his face. Well, join the crowd . . . if he insisted on playing around in her dreams, she was glad he looked as tired as she felt.

"Yes, did you?"

"You want to talk about the weather now?" he snapped.

Ellie stopped in her tracks and faced him with a look of surprise. Color rushed to her face. Okay, so her ears were still ringing from the warning the mayor's wife had delivered.

After several hours of mulling over the incident, she decided the woman's words had been intended as a warning. She appreciated the tip, but it made her mad too. She was trying to fit in here. But Sam didn't know about that conversation, so what had singed his tail feathers?

"What about the weather?"

He turned from a couple of strides ahead of her and sighed. "Sorry . . . are you organized for Saturday?"

Ellie waved the sign. "Thanks to Marge, these signs should be ready by tomorrow." Several long steps brought her to his side. "That's all I have to do: pass out the signs . . . and bake something."

"You want to get dinner?"

Ellie's heart tripped into overdrive. Dinner? With Sam? Oh, yes, she wanted to spend time with him. "Thanks, but I need to get back to work." But she didn't dare. Not when he looked like he needed someone to take care of him. Her chest tightened as if she'd been squeezed into a corset. It wasn't that she didn't want to spend time with Sam. She did. She wanted more than he offered. It was better to put some distance between them. And protect him from town gossip.

"I had several new customers come in today."

Friday morning, Ellie crashed through the door to Sam's office, gripping a bulging grocery bag to her chest. "I need to use your oven," she huffed, leaning against his desk. Too late she realized he was on the phone.

Sam held up a hand as he spoke to the caller. "And

you're taking care of all the arrangements?" He frowned and grabbed a pencil, then scribbled something on paper. "The food? Uh-huh—"

Ellie froze, suddenly realizing what his conversation was about.

"A tent?" The pencil in his hand snapped in half. "Okay, okay . . . I'll leave it all to you. What?" He looked at Ellie and made a face. "Yes, there's room." He scribbled again. "What? No, Aaron—" Clutching the phone with white knuckles, Sam jumped to his feet. "Today? No! Absolutely not! I can't—"

Sam fell back in his chair. "Look, I can't, I have—" Pinching the skin between his eyes, he sighed. "Okay, but . . . right . . . right . . . bye."

Slamming the phone down, he looked up. "Any chance you could spend the day at my house? A landscaper is coming to get the lawn ready for the party."

"What?"

"Yep!" He ran his hand around the back of his neck and sighed. "That was Shawn's agent! We're not to worry about a thing . . . except inside the house. The agent is covering everything!" His brows arched almost to his hair. "Including, get this, painting the outside of the house."

"You're kidding, right?"

Sam shrugged. "Anyway, what can I do for you?"

"Oh!" Ellie looked down at the grocery bag clutched in her arms. "I can't bake in that toy oven in the loft. May I use your kitchen to cook for the bake sale?" She didn't have time to worry about gossip, not if she intended to meet her obligations to her new hometown.

Sam's head jerked up. "Today?"

"Yes," she answered, half afraid he would jump on her from across the desk, and half hoping he would. "If that's okay?"

Sam rounded the desk, gave her a big hug, and swung her and the groceries around with a laugh. "That would be great!" He set her on her feet and swooped to drop a quick kiss on her startled mouth. Then he took the grocery bag from her numb arms. "Let's go. The landscaper is supposed to be there any minute."

Hours later, Ellie twirled around Sam's kitchen, humming and cleaning the countertops to a shine. The chocolate-chip cookies were finished, the cream cheese pound cake was in the oven, and she still had an hour before lunch.

Her voice rang out the words of the song that skimmed around in her head as she moved to survey the dining room. It might be a push, but she was confident she could have the room painted by the time Sam came home.

After that kiss, she could probably paint the whole house and keep going. A dreamy smile stretched across her face as she opened the can of paint.

Oh, yeah, Sam's kiss was the perfect way to start the day. It was a good thing she'd insisted on stopping by the hardware store to pick up paint before she made the trip out here. Look at all the time she would have wasted. Sam had met with the landscapers before she arrived. All she had to do was get ready for the bake sale tomorrow, and paint!

Sometime after six, Sam banged through the back door, carrying a large pizza box. "What happened to the front yard?" His voice sounded like a snarl.

"Oh, you're home!" Ellie gulped.

"I'm not sure this is my house." Sam plopped the aromatic box on the counter and stalked toward the front door. "When I left, I had a crumbling sidewalk in the overgrown lawn!" His voice echoed off the living room walls as he stomped to the front door. "Now, I have—"

"A circle drive around a birdbath and lily pond!" Ellie eyed the pizza box longingly as she dried the last paintbrush and followed Sam.

"What the—" The ancient door banged against the hinges as Sam caught sight of the scraped dirt in front of the house.

"You don't have to yell, I'm right here." She almost barreled into his back, he stopped so fast. "You didn't notice that I painted the dining room."

Sam turned an incredulous gaze toward her. "Paint?" He made it sound like a dirty word. "You expect me to notice paint when the whole front yard has been destroyed?" Mumbling and shaking his head, he shoved the screen door out of his way and stalked out.

Following on his heels, Ellie glanced around and sighed. The porch was just as she'd pictured. Deep shade made the swing and old rocking chairs look like a haven from the day's troubles. From the set of Sam's shoulders and the muscles jumping along his jaw, she wasn't sure how much shelter the porch provided.

Clearing her throat, she said, "It'll look better in a couple of days, after they lay the sod—"

Sam whirled toward her. "What sod?" His eyes seemed to spit green sparks as his glance jumped from her face to the piles of red dirt and back. "Who said anything about sod? Or tearing up my yard . . . or putting in a lily pond?"

Ellie shuddered as his voice echoed off the tin roof of the porch and sidestepped a couple of feet. "Um, well, um . . . Larry, the um, landscaper, um . . . came to get a drink of water . . . and we started talking." She shrugged, her gaze darting away from the fury on his face to rest on the mounds of red dirt. "Well, it sounded perfect when the landscaper described how it would look."

Sam looked her up and down, his hands on his hips, his brows arched to his hair, his lips stretched flat across his teeth. "This was your idea?" His voice was a near whisper. His left arm gestured toward the torn-up earth. "The half-circle drive, the birdbath . . . the lily pond . . ." His gaze darted back and forth from the lawn to her face with each word. "All this was your idea?"

Ellie squared her shoulders and took a deep breath, ready to explain. Before she could speak, anger coursed through her. Why was he upset? The yard couldn't look any worse. Tilting her chin, her hands planted on her hips in a stance that mirrored his, she met the hot emotion flaring in his eyes.

"Not at first." She inhaled with a shudder, but Sam's mouth opened, so she rushed to finish before he got the wrong idea. "I don't know much about these things. But Larry the landscaper explained the potential this house and yard had." She shrugged. "I thought . . . it sounded great!" Ignoring the slash of red highlighting his cheek and the heat in his glare, she grinned. "I think a birdbath would be wonderful to watch from this porch."

There, let him do his worst! So she was a dreamer. If he didn't like the plans . . . he could tell the landscaper tomorrow. Her gaze clung to his face, dark with afternoon shadow along his jaw and tense with surprise. For the first time she noticed the shadows of fatigue under his dark eyes.

"Sam, I—"

"Ellie Gray, you are full of surprises." He swung back to face her after another look at the yard. "You really think it will look good?"

Ellie choked on the rest of her apology. "Y-you aren't mad?"

His tension melted away. His body seemed to float toward her, until the toes of his boots touched her tennis shoes. His hand, rough from work, lifted, and he ran his fingers from the center of her forehead through the edge of her hair to stop with a gentle cupping of her jaw. Watching the darkening shadows in her green eyes, he lowered his lips to hers in a whisper of a kiss.

That's all it was, a brush of lips, a moment of skin against skin, but her lips tingled with energy as he lifted his head.

"No, I'm not mad." Sam held her chin for a moment

longer. Need and energy grew inside him. He sighed. "We should eat the pizza before it gets cold!"

He ought to be mad! Sam pulled the front door to with a gentle touch. He ought to be furious. From the moment he had first laid eyes on Ellie Gray, his world had turned upside down.

This was the final straw. Standing there on the porch, looking deep into green eyes filled with hope and longing he felt the last of his defenses crumble. Despite his plans for the future, or his need to prove himself, he accepted defeat.

His battle to keep Ellie out of his heart was over. It had been from the moment he saw her, he suspected. Now he was admitting the truth. He'd fallen head over heels in love with her.

No matter what it took, he was going to win Ellie's heart.

Another Friday night came and he was still painting. Three bake sales and farmers' markets had passed, each more successful than the last. Saturday morning in downtown Redbud was a hive of activity. Women preened with pride over the demand for their baked goods. Each week the number of farmers attending the market increased.

Even the kinds of things for sale increased. Crafts, flowers, and canned goods joined the display of fresh vegetables. Ellie's idea was a success. Her popularity with the townfolk didn't take her attention away from the job. In fact, Sam expected the painting to be finished in another week, as they were only concentrating on the rooms that would be used for the party. That included the guest suite and den on the second floor, where Shawn and Dawn would stay.

Even with their progress, Sam started measuring time by how many walls they painted. Most nights he dropped into bed too exhausted to hold his eyes open. Which was good. He spent too many waking hours thinking about Ellie.

Everything had changed. Let people drag his name around town like a worn-out puppy. He had survived the past with all the talk about his grandfather. If people wanted to talk, let them. All he cared about was protecting Ellie and sealing the deal with Shawn. If that made him less than honorable, he'd face the consequences. Until he owned that land, he had nothing to offer her.

He glanced across the room to where Ellie sat on the floor, painting white trim around a window. Less than a month ago, she had been a stranger.

His attraction to her grew by the day. But his hands were tied. He couldn't start a relationship with someone like Ellie unless he had serious intentions. His main concern was acquiring this land. After that, he wanted a real life with a wife and kids, but he had no guarantees. He couldn't take that big step to seal a relationship until he dealt with his cousin.

This could be another of Shawn's pranks. Sam's hand shook, leaving more paint on the roller than he needed as his thoughts played havoc with his emotions. Seeing the blob of blue he left on the wall, he cast a quick glance at Ellie before painting over the mess he'd made.

He knew he was backing away from involvement,

but thoughts of her had taken over his life. Okay, so his days weren't all work. He hadn't expected to enjoy painting. Painting walls seemed tame to a man used to wrestling a chain saw while controlling a bucket truck.

He enjoyed a sense of satisfaction when he trimmed a tree to perfection. But he had also experienced a sense of accomplishment by adding new life to his house with each coat of fresh paint.

Ellie wasn't the cause of his newfound sense of contentment. Ha! Who was he trying to kid?

As if she'd read his mind, she looked up. "How's the painting going?"

"Another blasted streak."

"A job worth doing is worth doing well." The mischievous glint in her eyes and her singsong tone took the sting out of her words.

"You heard that a lot, did you?" His brow arched in question as he glanced in her direction.

"More than you could ever know."

The glint of humor in her eyes dulled. Her grin disappeared. Sam wondered about her past. "What was it like growing up with two old maids?"

She was sitting on the floor, her shoulders hunched low over one leg as she painted the baseboard. After long moments of silence, he decided she wasn't going to answer and turned back to the paint the Carolina blue wall, letting her silence fill the room.

"It was a lot like boarding school, I guess."

Sam made a quick swipe to paint over the squiggly line he'd made at the sound of her voice. "That good, huh?"

"It wasn't bad." The blue bandanna tied over her hair

hid her expression. "It was like always being a guest—maybe more like being an extra—in someone's house."

He looked back. She wasn't hunched over now. Her back was straight as the door frame.

"That's . . . uh . . . an interesting way to describe it." He searched for a topic to lighten the conversation. "Hey, you know what tomorrow is—Ben! Ben, no!" He dropped the paint roller and made a grab for the cat. "Don't do that! Shoo, cat. Get away!"

"What's wrong? What's Benny doing?" Ellie spun around to see why he was shouting. The sight of Sam and Ben took her breath away. Laughter bubbled in her chest. The scene would have been perfect for a slapstick comedy.

Ben had swiped his long plumed tail against the wall Sam had just painted. Long, uneven trails in the wet paint looked like a modern art design on the wall.

Ellie pressed her wrist against her mouth to smother her giggles and blinked tears from her eyes. Sam's repeated attempts to catch Benny reminded her of old Three Stooges movies. He stood frozen in place. His eyes darted from the wall to the cat to his right hand. A handful of paint revealed his attempt to catch Benny by the tail.

Ellie couldn't believe her eyes. She watched Benny wrap around Sam's legs, his tail leaving stripes of blue paint on the denim jeans with each swipe. Sam's mouth dropped open. He stared from the wiggling cat with a blue tail to his hand covered in blue paint.

A choked sound escaped Ellie's lips as she met Sam's incredulous stare. His expression caused her to lose control, and her giggles erupted. She couldn't decide what was more amusing, Sam's look of amazement or Benny's tail standing tall in a blue spike.

Sam tore his glance from her and met the cat's unblinking gaze. He glanced to where Ellie had fallen back on the floor, shaking with laughter. A rumble started deep in his chest. His laughter mingled with hers as Benny stared.

"Ben, you sure know how to make things interesting."

"And more work." Ellie wiped tears from her eyes. "I need to wash the paint off his tail before he tries to clean himself up."

"I'll hold him." Sam held up his blue hand. "Maybe I can get cleaned up too."

Ellie fell back in another fit of giggles. "You look like a Smurf!"

Sam struggled to keep a straight face as he moved to stand over her, his fake frown just one wrinkle less than a grin.

"Then you'd better help me clean this mess up if you don't want to look like that little girl Smurf."

Ellie choked on a new wave of laughter as she struggled to her feet. Picking up the offended cat, she murmured, "You mean Smurfette?"

"Whatever!" Sam led the way out of the room. He'd laughed more in the last month than he had in his whole life. Ellie brought this old house to life. "Can you wash a cat?"

She followed Sam through the master bedroom. Benny needed a bath before the paint started to dry. Being stuck in the bathroom with Sam seemed strange.

So was being in his bedroom, she thought, as she darted an inquisitive glance around his private space as he led the way to the bath.

Everything in the room shouted male. There were no frills, no pictures on the dresser or the nightstand. Still, something reached out to her, making her insides twist in a way she wasn't familiar with.

"I don't know. I've never tried to give him a bath. Benny's a free spirit. He mostly does as he pleases."

While Sam ran water in one of the two sinks, Ellie gave the room a quick look. This wasn't an ordinary bath. From the spaciousness of the room, she guessed it had once been a small bedroom. The bathtub was enormous. There was a separate shower and lots of storage space in the closet Sam opened.

"Use this old towel. No sense in ruining a new one with paint."

"You'd better wash your hands first." She gripped the squirming cat tighter. "We don't want any more surprise painting. I can just imagine Ben leaving a trail of blue across your furniture."

"It wouldn't hurt anything." Sam frowned at her start of surprise, realizing he'd spoken the truth. He wasn't emotionally attached to the furnishings. Not like he was to the house. That seemed strange. "It's just stuff to get by with."

Chapter Ten

"**B**ut . . . I thought this furniture belonged to your grandparents." Ellie turned the wriggling cat so his head was facing Sam. "Hold him behind his front legs, and don't let go." She lowered the stiff blue tail to the sink full of water. "He's not going to like this. I hope he doesn't scratch you." As she spoke she splashed water at Ben's fast-twitching tail.

"Hurry! He's squirming to get away. Holding an unwilling feline isn't one of my skills." Sam struggled for a better grip. "Are you growling?"

"Not me." Ellie tried not to laugh as the cat growled louder. "Ben doesn't seem to like taking a bath. I warned you."

"Okay, I get the message." Sam rearranged his grip on the wimpering mass of fur. "Can you hurry? I don't want to hurt him." His words ended in a grunt. "He's really squirming."

"Don't let him scratch you." She felt the heat of Sam's body as he shifted to hold the cat. Great! That's all she needed. Her cat smeared with paint and a man who smelled like a page out of *GQ* magazine. "Hang on! I have to get the paint off. He'll get sick if he licks it." Ummm . . . that was powerful aftershave, all male and . . . stimulating. "I can't believe this paint is drying with all this water!"

Sam pressed against the back of her leg, trapping her against the cabinet.

Ellie bit down on her lip to contain a groan as she tried to wash Benny's tail and look back at Sam at the same time. Not an easy task with Benny swatting his tail like a wildcat.

Sam groaned.

She tried to glance over her shoulder. "Why are you lying on Benny's head? Did he hurt you?"

"No! Hurry!"

His voice sounded muffled, as if he had a mouthful of cotton. She didn't pause to look again. The furious growls coming from Benny's throat escalated in volume. She'd been the target of Ben's claws and knew the damage he could do without trying. She grabbed the whipping tail for one last splash. "There, I think that's most of it. The rest should come off when I dry him."

As she reached for the towel, Sam let out a groan. His weight crushed her against the cabinet, warming her with the heat from his body. Energy sizzled through her, making her want to echo the sound that came from low in his throat. If only—

"Ow!"

"Sam?" Ellie twisted around enough to see his face buried against Ben's neck and head. "Are you all right?"

He groaned again.

"Here! Give him to me. You can dry his tail." Ellie reached for Ben. "Sam! Are you biting my cat's ear?" Her shriek bounced off the ceramic walls, echoing her amazement and startling the angry cat.

Sam lifted a fur-filled mouth. He tried to hold the cat, spit cat hair out of his mouth, and change positions with her.

"I was holding his ear between my lips." He sounded defensive, but it had been an act of desperation. That feline devil had shredded the underside of his arms from elbow to wrist.

"Why would you bite his ear . . . even with your lips?" Ellie spotted the red marks on his arms. Angry slashes streaked his skin, some spouting drops of blood, others just red and raw. "Sam, I'm sorry." Ellie vacillated between needing to dry the cat and wanting to hold Sam.

"No problem!" Sam ran a soothing hand over the cat's head. "Poor old fellow, he tried not to scratch me, even when he panicked." The big cat purred and nudged his head into the comfort of Sam's touch. "Good boy."

Her insides started to melt. Tears filled her eyes. How many men would put up with a cat's claws and scratches just so the cat could be protected from harm? Sam was one in a million.

Every time she managed to find something wrong with him, he did something that warmed her heart and made her dream foolish dreams. She was in trouble!

Sam wasn't like anyone she'd ever known. He made her laugh, even when they were working. He made her want things she had never dared admit before.

Okay, her defenses were low. She'd been missing sleep for the past month. "Sam, I'm sorry." She dropped Benny and grabbed his arm. "Do you have a first-aid kit?"

"I'm okay." He nodded toward the sputtering cat stalking around the bathroom as he reached to close the bedroom door. "Check Ben out. Be sure I didn't hurt him."

"I can't believe you bit his ear." Ellie buried her laughter in the back of Benny's neck after making sure there wasn't any damage to his ears. "Poor Benny. He's never had a human bite him before." She leaned against the counter, shaking with laughter.

Sam glanced up from washing droplets of blood off his arm. Most of the damage was superficial. The skin wasn't broken, except for a few spots where Ben's claws had dug in. It wasn't his cat injury he was worried about, but the way he responded to Ellie.

Her face glowed in the soft light. Her lips twitched as she tried to hold a straight face. Her eyes sparkled with humor.

Sam growled deep in his throat, similar to the sound Benny had made just minutes earlier.

Ellie dropped the protesting feline and leaned back against the counter as Sam moved close.

He had started this as a joke. But the sparkling green of her eyes mirrored the heat in his gut, and he was lost.

He cupped her face with both hands. His heart

pounded. He watched the throbbing pulse in her throat and then he knew. Ellie felt the same madness he did.

And it was madness. Still, he couldn't help brushing his lips across hers.

Her chest heaved against his. Her breath escaped in a moan as his lips sealed hers with a kiss. He had wanted to kiss her again ever since the wedding ceremony. But with each kiss, he wanted more. He needed to know if she tasted as sweet as he remembered.

When thoughts of her kept him awake at night, when she danced through his every waking moment, he needed to know that kissing her was as good as he'd dreamed it would be.

It was better. Her lips trembled under his like a leaf shuddering in the breeze. He froze. Half of him was afraid she would stop before he got his fill of her sweetness. The other half of him prayed she would stop before he lost control.

Then he had his reward. With a tentative move that brought her fully into his arms, she leaned against him. This time, when he felt the moist warmth of her lips brush against his, he lost all conscious thought. With a moan that he could have sworn she echoed, he wrapped her in his arms and pressed his lips to hers.

One second he was aware of holding a desirable woman in his arms, the next, he was conscious only of Ellie's touch. Her lips melted under his. Their tongues danced in a rhythm as old as man, and as new as each kiss. Warmth flowed through him as a sense of rightness raced through his mind. This was the woman he'd been . . .

Benny landed on the counter with a screech that jolted them apart. The furious cat skidded on the wet countertop and landed in the sink full of water. He lunged out of the water with a howl that sounded suspiciously like a dirty word.

Water splashed over Ellie and Sam, bringing them back to reality.

Ellie sprang away from the embrace, brushing at the water dripping from her clothing. She watched as Sam stared from his soaked jeans to the dripping cat. The indignant noises from Ben's throat released the tension that twisted her insides. The look of disbelief on Sam's face offered her an escape. She started laughing.

Saved by the cat.

Thank goodness for Ben. One minute she'd been on the brink of a passion she'd never known; the next instant, she'd been splashed back to reality by her big lovable cat.

Ellie arrived early the next morning.

"Grab a cup of coffee, I made omelets." Sam glanced up from his seat at the table as her tentative steps carried her through the back door. "We need to get going."

Ellie reached for a cup, thankful for the excuse to turn her back on him as memories from the night before flashed in her head.

The cat and paint incident had cost them precious time the night before. Despite the progress they had made on the house, the date for Shawn's party loomed over their heads, so they had worked late. Sam offered her the use of the guest room so they could get an early start.

"I can't stay here," she said, memory of Pauline Morgan's warning still clear in her mind.

"It's late, you're exhausted."

She concentrated on washing the last brush and frowned. His offer was tempting, but with renewed strength, she crossed the room. "I'm tired, but I can't risk being the target of all that small-town gossip you've warned me about."

Sam froze at the tartness of her tone. Paint supplies littered the floor around him, waiting to be cleaned. They worked late, trying to escape the awkwardness of the kissing session in the bath.

As a result of their nonstop painting frenzy, another room was finished. But he was exhausted. He knew from the dark circles under her eyes that Ellie was too.

Still, the word *gossip* stopped his objections to her plan to return to town for the night. Despite the innocence of their situation . . . he admitted she was right. No matter how tired she was or how early they intended to start, she couldn't spend the night.

But Benny could.

Ellie liked getting up bright and early on Saturday morning, especially today. She needed more fabric for curtains. The store in town had the material on back order, but she was running out of time. Sam suggested a trip to a large fabric store in Mt. Airy. Afterwards, they could hit the flea markets.

Her yawn was part sigh as she poured the steaming coffee in her cup. Their plans had made sense last night when she'd been too tired to think . . . but now, after another night without sleep, she wasn't so sure she should spend more time with Sam.

Early morning light bathed his face. His dark hair sparkled with dampness from his shower. The scent of his aftershave stimulated her senses more than coffee.

How could she do this? How could she spend time with Sam and keep her feelings hidden?

"Are you sure you can spare the time? I feel guilty. I know you try to work around home on Saturday."

"You think I'd miss an excuse to go to the flea markets? Are you kidding?" His grin reminded her of their previous trip. "After the luck I had last Sunday afternoon?" He waggled one arched brow in the playful manner that always caused her to laugh. "I wouldn't miss this for anything."

"Oh? You're looking for more andirons? How many fireplaces does this house have anyway?"

"Get serious, woman. That purchase was just the beginning." Sam winked, pretending he didn't notice the dark circles under her eyes. So he wasn't the only one to lose sleep last night. That was good to know. This thing between them had to be settled, sooner or later. With the memory of her lips still fresh in his head, he would settle for later. "Are you forgetting the dream-catcher I bought for the den?"

Ellie giggled. "Does it work? Have you had any dreams since you brought it home?"

"Funny you should ask." Sam gave her a look from under an arched brow. Despite the tired look around her eyes, color flooded her face.

So she was affected by their brush with emotion. He hated the tension between them this morning. Being with Ellie made him realize there were important things in life besides work and possessions.

"Speaking of dreams, you don't look as if you slept very much. Are you sure you want to go today?"

Ellie lifted the fork to her mouth and willed her hand steady. In slow motion, she started to chew. She wasn't ready for this, not now. Maybe . . . later.

But Sam's sharp look demanded an answer.

"I was worried . . . about Benny."

Sam gave a snort as he looked down. The ugly red welts had faded to traces of red lines on his arms. Here and there, dark scabs marked the spots where Benny's claws had punctured the skin. Compared to some of the injuries he got on the job, this was nothing.

"You should be worried about me."

"I'm sorry. I forgot! How are your scratches?"

"About time." His grin lifted one corner of his mouth. "I'm the injured party here."

"Right!" Ellie tried for a teasing tone despite the thudding in her chest. Then, remembering the way Sam had looked with fur hanging from his lips, she laughed. "Since you bit my cat, I'm worried that you haven't had your rabies shots." She looked around the room. Crumbs littered the floor around the food bowl. "Where is Benny?"

"Very funny!" Sam's lips twitched. "Your precious cat went hunting." He nodded toward the open back door.

"Oh, no!" Laughter shivered though her, making it impossible to keep a straight face. "Does he bring you presents?" Sam's glare almost made her laugh out loud. "When did he start that?"

Sam grinned. "A couple of days ago. Couldn't you train him to bring in something more appetizing?"

Ellie laughed but quickly covered her face with her hands to hide the rush of tears. Relief, that's all it was. Benny bringing dead offerings to people he liked was nothing new. She needed this release from the tension she had felt since their kisses last night.

"He's not a big-game hunter, you know." A giggle escaped. "You're the one who insisted I bring him along. What did he leave for you?"

"A couple of lizards, a mouse, and a mole," he said. His insides caved in relief as she laughed. Ellie looking tired he could handle . . . but tears?

"Benny's very particular. You should feel proud he likes you."

"Yeah, I feel real special when I have to clean a dead carcass off the doorstep." Sam's pained expression brought on another bout of giggles. Then he said, "But as a foot warmer, he's hard to beat."

Ellie gasped. "He slept on your bed?"

Sam's eyes glowed with a light she didn't trust. "Yep!"

"I-I'm sorry." Ellie didn't know whether to laugh or run for safety.

Sam drained his coffee cup. "Don't worry about it, I could get used to that little motor of his." He nodded to her empty plate. "Are you about ready to leave?"

"I can't leave Benny outside."

"Why not?" Sam watched worry lines return to her face. "He's been here often enough. He usually spends time outside. What's different now?"

"I'm afraid he'll get lost." Ellie lifted her chin. "He's new here, you know. I let him out. But I check on him."

"He's a cat. He knows how to take care of himself." He hadn't intended causing her to worry about the cat. "He'll be okay. Come on, we won't be gone long."

"I don't know." Ellie put her plate in the dishwasher, then went to look out the back door.

"Here," Sam said as he passed her a bowl of water. "Put that on the back porch. He'll be fine until we get home."

Home. That one word, along with his kindness about her cat's safety, almost brought Ellie to tears. But she held them back. She was determined to enjoy what time she had left with Sam. Her work on the house was almost done. Not even his casual reference to their returning home would put a damper on this day, if she could help it.

One thing she had learned early: there was no need to cry over what had already happened. The elderly sisters had insisted she accept her life and make the best of her resources. She owed Emiline and Anastasia a debt of gratitude. Without their guidance, how would she have managed to shove her disappointment aside and cherish every remaining moment spent with Sam?

"You think he'll be all right? He won't get lost?"

"He's roamed this place for days."

"Okay, I'll just freshen up and grab my pocketbook."

"Pocketbook?"

Ellie's face flamed with color. Turning from stacking the dishwasher, she glared at him. "That's what the old—"

". . . ladies called a purse." Sam finished her sentence.

Ellie met his look for long moments. Energy surged between them. How had they gotten to the point where he could finish her thoughts? Emotion filled her until she felt as if she would explode if he didn't say something.

Did he know what he did to her? Did he suspect she had fallen for him? What was going on behind the fire in his hazel eyes?

She struggled to control the panic threatening to envelop her and tried to grin. Her face felt stiff, as if tears had dried on skin that would crack if she moved. But her lips stretched, imitating a smile as she fought to regain control.

"Is that what your grandmother called her purse?"

Deep slashes lined his cheeks as he gave an answering grin. "Yeah."

"Oh, well, I'll just be a minute!" She dashed for the door, glad of an excuse to get away from Sam. He looked sleepy, like a big cat waking up from a nap.

She didn't want to think about his sleeping habits. She'd almost lost it when he mentioned finding Benny in his bed. Just for a beat, she imagined herself there with Sam and the cat. The images raced around in her head like a movie clip, inciting reactions from every part of her body and filling her face with heat.

Five minutes later, she returned to the kitchen and found Sam on his knees, rubbing Benny's head. The sight of his washed-out jeans stretched across his perfect backside didn't help her gain control of her wayward thoughts.

Her gaze clung to his back. A green T-shirt outlined every muscle in soft cotton but hung loose at the waist.

Running her hand along the kitchen counter, she clamped her lips on the urge to tell him how much she enjoyed spending time with him. Memories of his kiss, of the way her body melted against his, kept her silent. She liked spending time with Sam too much for her own good.

Sam watched Ellie's long denim-clad legs disappear down the hall and drew his first deep breath since she'd settled into the chair across the table. Blood pounded in his ears from just thinking about the past few minutes. But it was the images racing through his mind that taunted him, like how her hair looked darker when it was still damp from her shower.

A loud *meow* jerked his thoughts away from Ellie. He moved to let Ben in the kitchen door. He'd lost enough sleep last night thinking about the kisses they exchanged. He didn't need fresh images to set him on edge.

But she was back before he could clear his head. Even with his back turned, he knew the instant she walked in the room. Giving the cat's head one final rub, he prepared for the next encounter.

"Ben's back, safe and sound." Standing, he turned to watch her slow ramble along the cabinets.

"Ummmm."

What was bothering her? She'd seemed happy

enough when she first arrived. "Are you ready to go? We have a lot to do today."

"Sam . . ." Her green eyes stared from across the room. "Can I ask you something?"

"Sure," he said. Tension clutched his insides as he leaned a shoulder against the door. From the look on her face, he was afraid he knew what she was going to say. She wanted out of the job. He took a deep breath. "Ask away." What was the point in dragging things out? Spit it out and go on, that was his motto.

"I . . . uh . . . was wondering." Ellie's gaze darted around the room before returning to meet his glance.

Uh-oh, here it comes. Funny, he'd thought she had more spunk. If she wanted to leave, he couldn't stop her. But there was one other thing. How could she run a business if she ran away from a job when things got tough?

It was his fault. He'd made the move to kiss her. All she had cared about was washing paint off her cat. At least, that's what he thought until the moment her lips melted under his.

Was she running scared?

He was determined to keep their situation from getting out of hand. He knew what small towns were like. People never forgot a tidbit of news about their neighbors. It might even be too late. He'd heard a comment or two about Ellie working at his house.

If there was any way to prevent his name from being dragged through the gossip mill, he intended to find it. He'd lost hours of sleep last night thinking about Ellie.

Having her in his house, hearing her talk to Benny, reminded him of what he was missing, of what he dreamed about for the future. But he would survive. He'd do anything necessary to achieve his ambition. But at what price?

"This might be personal, but I was wondering." A slow grin washed some of the strain from her face. "All this furniture, did it belong to your grandmother?"

Air whooshed out of his lungs. Sam shook his head to clear the buzzing in his ears. Had he heard her right? Was she asking him about furniture? He thought she wanted to quit. Sam shook his head. Women! Who could figure them out?

"Yeah . . . most of it was Granny's. Some of it was my mother's." Sam waved his hand to encompass the house. "Why?" Her question didn't make sense.

Ellie's eyes sparkled like gems in a spotlight. She darted to the old-fashioned hutch and grabbed one of his grandmother's dinner plates, then rushed to his side.

"So, this plate with these delicate little pink flowers, this was your grandmother's? She passed it on to you?"

"Yeah, she left everything to me." Sam frowned. Her face glowed as if a spotlight burned inside her head. "Why?"

Ellie rubbed the plate as if she were trying to feel the design. "Grandmothers would like stuff like this, wouldn't they?"

"I guess—"

"You're so lucky." Ellie shook his arm. Excitement sparkled out of her eyes. "You have things that belonged to your family." She stared dreamily down at the plate. "It must feel good to know about your past."

His mouth opened, but her blazing eyes and the smile on her face held him speechless. The urge to drop a kiss on the enchanting curve of her lips was strong. Something held him back.

What could he say?

Suddenly he knew where this was going. Ellie wasn't backing out of the job.

Oh, no, it was worse. Thoughts of kissing her turned his blood to ice. He realized the truth. Ellie wanted to make a home for herself. He wasn't sure he liked the idea one little bit.

This job was temporary. It didn't matter that she'd done a good job, or how natural she looked in his house, or how right having her around seemed. He couldn't let her get her hopes up.

Despite Shawn's dare, when this land deal was completed he wanted to start a family. Once the deed was signed and the land was in his name, he'd have something to offer. Until then, he couldn't make promises, especially to someone like Ellie.

She didn't know about Shawn's dare, or about Sam's dreams. She wasn't interested in a family. All she talked about was making a success of her business. He admitted the truth. He was attracted to her. Once this job was over, she would move on. And he wanted more.

He had tried to help her because Shawn had taken advantage of her in a way he couldn't ignore. Was he fooling himself? Was it already too late to walk away from Ellie? This situation wasn't as simple as he'd thought.

"I see."

"No, really, think about it." She paced in front of him. "This stuff belonged to your grandmother. Wherever she is, my grandmother would have something similar, right?" She rubbed her hand across the plate again. A dreamy look crossed her face. "I'll shop around the flea markets, find things my grandmother would have liked." Grinning wide, cheeks dimpled, she glanced at him with eyes as bright as Christmas. "What do you think?"

"I think . . ." He swallowed the lump threatening to block his throat. The expectant look on her face and her wistful grin sent a shaft of pain twisting through his chest.

He couldn't tell her. He couldn't say he thought she was one of the most beautiful women he'd ever seen. He didn't dare. She would think he was crazy.

Maybe he was. But when she looked at him with her heart in her eyes, with that expression on her face, something inside him melted.

Sweat popped out on his forehead. He couldn't handle this female stuff. His grandmother never acted like this, or talked like this . . . but she'd never been homeless, either.

He looked in her sparkling eyes and felt his heart swell in his chest. "I think . . . I think you've got it all wrong, Ellie." His voice cracked almost like the grin leaving her face. He couldn't back down now. "You have your whole future to look forward to."

"But—"

Sam paused as confusion shadowed the brightness of her gaze. "Your past molded you into the woman you are today. You don't need to change that, but you should focus on your future." He almost choked on the words, afraid he'd given away too much, but he knew he was right.

"But you . . . live for the past." Ellie frowned, not sure what she wanted to say. She didn't want to hurt Sam's feelings, but he needed to follow his own advice. With a shuddering breath, she continued. "Everything you do is focused on recovering land and restoring your past."

Sam's jaw worked, but no sound came. Her words hit true as darts. Her message was as clear as the sky after a hurricane. Why hadn't he realized before? His gaze roved around the old-fashioned kitchen.

"I know." He met her glance, appreciating her courage. "That's how I know I'm right. Ellie, you don't need to know your history to be worth something. You proved your character with the choices you made, like moving to Redbud. People in this town didn't accept you because of your past. They like you for who you are."

His words echoed inside his head. Truth settled in the pit of his stomach like a boulder, leaving him wishing for the time he'd wasted. He hadn't looked past the obvious. It had taken Ellie's comments to open his eyes.

Of course people in small towns talked. It was their main form of entertainment. He'd had no more than his share of being discussed. Now that Ellie's words had opened his eyes, he understood.

He snapped out of a daze to see the confused look on her face. His efforts to keep Ellie safe, to keep her from being rejected by the locals, had been because he cared for her, not because he worried about past mistakes. The past was just that, days gone by.

Ellie was the woman he knew today because of her experiences, just as he was shaped by his past. Their parents and grandparents had done things that influenced who they were. How they reacted to those experiences was the important thing.

His shoulders heaved as he pulled cleansing air into his lungs. It was his first breath of his future. He was his own person, in charge of his choices.

"Ellie, you're right. You've made me see that the future is what's important."

She turned to him with an expression that was a mixture of wonder and dismay. "Can it be that easy? Can you forget about wanting to claim this land, about the gamble your grandfather took? Or Shawn's jokes?"

He shrugged. "Yes, I think I can. I won't claim it's going to be easy."

"What's different, Sam? What happened to make your need to buy back that land any less important?"

His heart lunged to his throat. He couldn't tell her the truth, not now. She wasn't ready. Picking his words carefully, he said, "I still want to buy this land. I won't deny that." He held her stare and felt his heart settle into a normal rhythm as he studied the toe of his boot. "But if I lost everything, I realize now, I could go on—"

"Sam! Don't—"

"I can't explain it, Ellie, but I could. Maybe it's the work we've put into this place, the time we've spent laughing while we worked . . . I don't know. But I've learned that people are more important than possessions."

"That's easy to say when you've got a family tree the size of a redwood." Ellie didn't like the anger in her voice, but she didn't like being patronized either. Sam was sweet to try to make her feel better. But she knew despite what he said, family was everything to him.

That's why kissing him and dreaming about him was a big mistake. She couldn't let herself forget that again. She didn't have a family tree. The sooner she finished this job and put some space between them, the better off she would be, even if it broke her heart to stay away from him.

"We'd better get going. If that fabric store doesn't have what I need, I won't be able to finish the curtains in time for the party."

Chapter Eleven

Sam glanced over at his passenger and the wiggling bundle of fur in her arms. Ellie's smile turned his insides upside down. They were almost home, but they couldn't get there soon enough to suit him. He'd heard nothing but crooning and silly nonsense since they left the flea market.

Haven't you ever wanted something so bad you'd do anything to get it? Sam tightened his grip on the steering wheel as Ellie's words circled his brain. It had been a week, but her innocent comment about the past had started this constant refrain in his head, almost as if his subconscious were sending him a message.

Easing his hand off the wheel, he felt for the key in his pocket. Yeah, he understood what she meant the moment the words left her mouth. His problem was that he had changed his mind. What he wanted now, with the desperation she'd described, was very different from what he'd imagined when she first said those words on the trip home from New York.

That's why he carried this bulky key in his pocket.

Another whimper from the puppy drew his attention. After a quick glance, he turned his attention back to the road and grinned. Getting the puppy had been his idea. Memory of the look on Ellie's face when she talked about his past haunted him, and made him wish things were different. One thing he could change about the past was having a pet.

He didn't know Ellie's plans. He didn't know what was going on in his own life. Like this key in his pocket. He'd taken possession of this key as a symbol of the past. He intended to give it to Ellie. But since they shared those earth-shaking kisses in his bathroom, he was more confused than ever.

"What are you going to name him?"

Sam flinched. The small red mutt sitting in her lap was his responsibility. What had he been thinking? He hadn't, that was the scary part. He had reacted to Ellie, to thoughts of a future with her. When they passed a man with puppies for sale, he grabbed the first one Ellie looked at. A quick glance at her lap gave him a view of round ears and a face too pitiful to describe.

"Droopy."

"What?"

"I'm going to name him Droopy." Sam nodded toward the handful of fuzz snuggled in her lap. "With a hangdog face like that, what else could you name the mutt?"

"Sam." Her rebuke ended in a giggle. "He does look

pitiful. With these long ears and this sad little face, he does look droopy." She rubbed the pup's head and murmured, "Droopy?"

Sam gave a snort as the puppy whined and wiggled his short body, twisting to get closer to the soft, crooning voice. "He's smarter than he looks, that's for sure."

"Of course he's smart." Ellie raised the dog in both hands and cuddled him close, resting her chin on the pup's head. "Look how calm he's been on the ride home."

With a pointed glance at her cuddling the dog, Sam decided he was better off not commenting on how lucky the animal was as he snuggled against her chest. He wasn't sure they were ready to deal with his revealing thoughts. One thing he did know: he was jealous of a blasted puppy.

"Here's another batch of cookies to wrap." Stella dropped the tray and whirled away. Even in jeans, she had almost as much flair as in her pink uniform, Ellie thought as she wrapped more cookies.

Tomorrow was a big day, the one-month anniversary of the bake sale and farmers' market. They were making a special effort for the big event. That's why she wasn't working on Sam's house, as she usually did on Friday nights.

"Hey, Ellie," Laura Riley huffed as she deposited a boxful of items on the table. "I've been meaning to ask you about a call we got for a big order of flowers." She turned to call to a woman across the room, "What's the date on them flowers, Della?"

"A month, tomorrow," Della said as she turned. "Is Sam throwing a party, Ellie?"

"That reminds me," Brandy said from across the room, where she was wrapping pies. "The bakery got a big order for that Saturday too."

"The diner did too," Stella said. "The order for Roy's spicy wings is so large we had to special order extra wings out of Raleigh."

"You wouldn't believe the ice cream order from the pharmacy," Colleen Swift said, then laughed. "Sam must be planning some celebration." Her inquisitive glance scanned the faces turned her way. A cunning look crossed her face. "Is he planning to make a special announcement or something?"

Ellie's stomach flipped over, filling her mouth with bile. One month, tomorrow. Her panic had nothing to do with her work. Most of the house was painted. Even the professionals hired to paint the outside of the house had pulled out yesterday. Since the landscapers had finished this week, all that was left were the final touches to the inside.

Then . . . she would lose her excuse to spend time with Sam.

She searched for a way to answer the questions aimed at her. But she couldn't reveal a word of what she knew. This wasn't her business. "I was hired to make curtains and paint."

"Right!" Terry Miller snickered as she said, "So, who's going to eat the ton of pizza ordered for that day?"

"Pizza?"

"Spicy wings . . . ice cream—"

"Don't forget all the cake from the bakery!"

"Sounds like—"

"A party!" Several voices chorused.

The door banged open as the mayor's wife whirled in, heels clicking as she crossed the floor. "Good, you're all here." She fanned herself with an ivory envelope. "Listen to this," she said excitedly. "This came in the afternoon mail for the skills auction, now listen." She paused dramatically. "As one of your items up for auction, please include dinner for two with Shawn Thorpe and his new bride." Glancing up, her eyes big as the cabbage roses on her dress, she demanded, "Can you believe it? Dinner with a movie star!"

"That's some prize—"

"We'll make a mint!"

Chatter filled the room. Ellie wrapped baked goods as fast as her hands would fly. What was Shawn up to now? Did Sam know about all this? Should she tell him?

It wouldn't hurt. Okay, be honest with yourself, you want to see him! Fighting against the little voices doing battle in her head, she was miles away when she heard her name called.

"Is it a party for Shawn and his bride, Ellie?"

"I—"

"A wedding reception," the mayor's wife said. "It's right here in our invitation."

After a collective gasp, a flurry of activity began. Hands flew as the women rushed to finish so they could go home. No doubt the mailbox would be the first thing they checked.

Ellie's shoulders slumped in relief. She didn't need to worry about keeping her mouth shut.

Funny—having everyone know your business, talk to you on the street, those things seemed good to her. Of course, she didn't have Sam's experience with the past. She didn't have to worry about what a grandfather had done to bring shame to the family name. Wrapping the last of the cookies, she sighed again.

Sam didn't have anything to be ashamed of. He was respected and liked by everyone. He was somebody to these people. He was one of them.

"Hey, Ellie?"

She turned toward the door. The mayor's wife and half a dozen other women were chatting. "In case we haven't told you, we're real happy you moved to Redbud."

Ellie's feet barely touched ground all morning. The biggest crowd yet attended the Saturday morning events downtown. But her happiness came from the words she had heard the night before.

She had made the right choice. Moving to Redbud was the best thing that had happened to her . . . next to meeting Sam. Emotion threatened to choke her as she thought about Sam, about the future.

When she had time to realize what this meant, her insides twisted. Redbud accepted her, at least, the female half of the population did. She had friends! What more could she ask?

Now that she had the acceptance of her adopted town, she realized it wasn't enough. Making something of herself was her dream, but she wanted more. She wanted Sam's approval, his love. Now that she had been accepted as part of this town, she had the confidence to let him know her feelings.

That's what she planned to do this very day! As soon as the bake sale was over—which wouldn't be long, as supplies were dwindling fast—as soon as she was finished here, she was going out to hang the last of the curtains at Sam's. Somehow, she intended to let him know how she felt about him.

All afternoon Ellie mulled over her next step as she put curtains up in the living room. When the doorbell rang, she frowned at the thought of another interruption to keep her from talking with Sam. Work first . . . that had seemed the best idea when she arrived earlier.

Now, several hours later, she was as jumpy as a cat. She had no idea how to tell Sam what she felt, or how he would react. Although, remembering the rapid beat of his heart as he held her the night they washed Benny, she was almost sure he shared her feelings. All she needed was a chance to tell him she had fallen in love with him.

Loud pounding on the door drew her back to the present. Where was Sam? Taking one last glance at the flowing white sheers against the lemon-yellow walls, she felt a sense of pride wash over her. The room looked great.

The doorbell pealed, and then more pounding on the door. Sam must still be painting upstairs, Ellie thought as she rushed to answer before the visitor knocked the door off the hinges.

"Oooh, it's you!" Startled, she fell back a step, clutching one hand to her chest as she stared at the man on the front porch. "Um . . . won't you come in?" Her voice squeaked. Meeting a famous movie star face to face wasn't something she'd experienced before. "I'll call Sa—"

"Hello, pretty lady. Who are you?" Shawn stopped by her side, took possession of her hand, and stared into her eyes.

"I'm, uh . . ." Ellie glanced over her shoulder, unsure how to explain. Where was Sam when she needed him? "I'm . . . the uh . . . substitute bride."

Shawn stared at her for long seconds, then threw his head back and laughed. The loud sound echoed off the walls, showing evidence of his vocal training—and scraping on her nerves.

Standing close enough to the star to see his five o'clock shadow and the hard glint in his eyes, Ellie realized the cousins didn't favor each other as much as she had thought. Shawn looked lean and edgy, while Sam . . . Sam was dependable—and exciting. Ellie stretched to look past the movie idol. "Where's—"

"Shawn?" Sam's surprised voice called from halfway down the stairs. "What are you doing here?"

"Hey, buddy!" Shawn's voice boomed. He glanced from Ellie to Sam with a big grin on his face. "I see you took my dare."

Ellie's heart thudded as she saw the look that turned Sam's face to a mask. *What dare?*

From Shawn's laugh and the suggestive nod in her

direction, she guessed his words had something to do with her. But what? Sam glared at his cousin. Shawn grinned. In a heartbeat, she realized which of the cousins she liked best. "What—"

"Where's Dawn?" Sam demanded over her stammer.

Ellie stood still as a mannequin as she watched the frozen expression on Sam's face. He took the last two steps in a measured pace, taking long seconds to glance in her direction. What she saw—or didn't see—in the frigid glint in his eyes scared her. What was going on?

"She's, uh—"

"Are you hungry?" Ellie intended to find out what Shawn was talking about. Especially since Sam didn't seem to want her to know. "We ordered pizza." Then she tossed a glare in Sam's direction, as if to say *so there, what are you going to do about that?*

She wasn't sure why she was angry, but she had a bad feeling about Shawn's laughing comment. After seeing Sam motion with his head as he'd tried to shush his cousin, she intended to find out what was going on.

All during the meal, Shawn carried on a one-man performance. He ate, laughed, talked, and generally tried to charm his audience of two.

Ellie admitted he was charming. Who wouldn't? Shawn was handsome, smooth in a way most men only dreamed of being—from his manners, to his easy adjustment, to their simple meal, which he seemed to enjoy.

Sam seemed just the opposite, uncomfortable, on edge even. He didn't look at Ellie when he thought she was looking at him.

Something was wrong. Something that involved Shawn, but how did it connect to her? From the moment he set eyes on Shawn, Sam hadn't acted like himself.

Taking a deep breath, Ellie said, "So, you and Sam have a dare?"

Shawn looked from her to Sam and laughed as he poked Sam in the shoulder. After a quick glance at Sam, Shawn turned his charm on Ellie. "I'm surprised he didn't tell you about the dare, so he could win."

It was amazing how the actor could project his voice. Cold chills ran down her spine as each word bounced off the walls.

"There was no need." Sam's commanding tone made the star's voice sound like a child's. "And there's no need now." Sam leveled a stare at his cousin for several seconds before turning to her. "Will you excuse us?" He barely spared her a glance as he jumped to his feet, almost knocking over his chair. He turned his stern gaze toward his cousin. "Shawn and I have some business to discuss."

"Ellie, the meal was delicious." Shawn grinned. "I haven't had pizza in a month."

His charm should have melted a heart of stone. But Ellie felt numb from the clipped tone of Sam's dismissal. Shawn's practiced charm did nothing for her. But she sensed he enjoyed Sam's discomfort more than his flirting with her. For the first time, she understood the competitive relationship between the cousins.

With his easy laugh and gloating expression, Shawn assumed he had the upper hand. Too bad he was competing with Sam. Ellie knew without a doubt which cousin she'd want on her side, even though she was angry with Sam.

Determination provoked her to forget good manners as she demanded, "Where is Dawn?"

"She . . . um . . . we—"

"Shawn, are you coming?" Sam barked from the hall.

Shawn gave a Gallic shrug, then turned to follow his cousin. Ellie stared after the movie heartthrob. Her brain hopped from one possibility to another. What was going on? Why was Sam so angry?

If she hadn't been frozen to her seat, she might not have heard the next words.

"You didn't tell Ellie about the dare, did you?"

"No!"

Ellie knew that tone. Sam spoke through gritted teeth.

". . . and I plan to keep it that way."

Ellie's brain swirled in confusion. Why shouldn't Sam tell her about a dare?

"Come on, buddy, everything worked out." Shawn laughed. "What's wrong with you? You got the girl. Now you get the land, free!"

The door slammed loud enough to tear it off the

hinges. Shawn's voice instantly replayed in her head. *You got the girl. Now you get the land, free!*

Bitterness filled her throat. Rushing to the sink, Ellie grabbed a glass of water. One swallow and she realized she had made the nausea worse. What could be worse than being the brunt of a dare?

Dishes clattered in her hands as she cleared the table. *Tend to your duties!* That's what she'd been taught by the elderly sisters. *Take charge of your life, no matter what the crisis. Stick to your routine. Take one step at a time . . . baby steps. You can handle anything, one step at a time.*

That theory got her as far as the hall. Muffled voices filtered through the door of Sam's study. But her thoughts were clearing. She couldn't be the brunt of a joke. She hadn't met Sam until the day of the wedding.

This dare wasn't an insult to her. But it could change Sam's life forever!

Gritting her teeth with the determination she'd been mustering all afternoon, she shoved the study door open. The cousins turned toward her, mouths open. Obviously she had interrupted an argument.

"Don't do it, Sam! Don't take the dare."

"Aw, Ellie!" Shawn's smooth tone made her feel about three years old. "You don't want him to lose, do you?"

Ellie whirled to face the actor like a mother defending her last chick. "Lose? No, I don't want him to lose." She marched to within a yard of the man who filled her every thought. "But you will lose, Sam, if you take his dare."

"How?" the actor scoffed.

Ellie didn't take her gaze off Sam. "You'll lose your self-respect. The pride that drove you to succeed will be dragged in the dust if you go along with his dare."

"What do you mean, his pride? I'm trying to give him back the land." Impatience coated Shawn's words. "I thought he wanted this place."

Ellie studied every feature on Sam's face before turning to glare at the actor. "He wanted to clear the family name, Shawn. But he can't, not this way—"

"Aw—"

"He won't!" Ellie insisted with one last glare at the star. Then she turned to Sam. "You've spent your life trying to make up for your grandfather's mistakes. Don't let this joke turn into a repeat of the past."

"He'd have the land, for crying out loud."

Ellie's gaze remained glued to Sam's. "He'd have the land, but what good are possessions if you don't have self-respect?"

"You aren't angry about the dare?" Sam murmured. "About being involved in all this?"

Her chest shuddered as she gulped for air. "You didn't know me when the dare—"

"I made the dare. He had nothing to do with it," Shawn snapped.

". . . so I'm not insulted," she finished.

"I should have told you—"

"Why? We were strangers. You didn't owe me explanations." Her glance encompassed the room. "But you owe it to yourself and all you've worked for, Sam. Stand up for what you believe in."

"He believes in his heritage, don't you get it?" Shawn waved his hand in a dramatic motion. "He's tried to buy this land since he made his first nickel."

One look at the emotions flitting across Sam's face and Ellie's shoulders sagged. Sam and Shawn were family. This wasn't any of her business. "I shouldn't have interrupted. I just—"

"Ellie, I—"

"He's trying to tell you he threw the offer back in my face. I don't know why. I'm trying to give the man's land back to him, and have a little fun. But he insists on a business deal." Slashes of red marked Shawn's cheeks. "I give up!"

Ellie backed toward the door. "I'd better go . . . let you finish. I'm . . . sorry I interrupted." She closed the door on her last word, staring at the wood panels while she clutched the doorknob.

She'd done it now! She'd stuck her nose in family business. Even if she didn't have a close connection to relatives, she knew better than to interfere. Too late now. She'd shown her feelings for Sam with that outburst.

And he had let her leave.

Okay, she had her answer. She needed to get away from here before she had to face Sam again.

"Don't go!"

Sam's voice ripped through her. She'd come to get Benny and say goodbye to the puppy. She'd been so busy telling herself all the reasons she should leave that she hadn't heard him come into the kitchen. She couldn't force herself to face him.

"Please, let me explain."

Didn't he know he was making this harder for her? She couldn't say goodbye like this. "You don't owe me explanations. I need to get going. It's late." One last pat to Droopy's head and she stood up.

"Let me apologize, at least."

Ellie shuddered. Benny objected to her sudden squeeze and wiggled out of her hands with a loud meow.

Relief bent Sam in half. He leaned to grip the back of a chair and took a deep breath. She wouldn't leave without her cat.

"I should have told you about the dare."

Her back to him, Ellie leaned against the sink. "It wasn't my business."

"It didn't seem important at the time." He stopped as her shoulders flinched. He let go of the chair and straightened. "We were strangers. I didn't see the need to reveal personal information." When she didn't respond, he sighed and ran his fingers through his hair. How could he make her understand? "I expected to drop you off at your shop and say good-bye."

If he hadn't been looking at her he wouldn't have seen her body twitch as if she'd taken a blow. Okay, he was being blunt, but he was telling the truth. He cleared his throat. "Except it didn't work the way I'd planned."

"You got saddled with me, you mean?"

Sam's heart thundered so hard he barely heard her low voice. At least she was talking to him. "No, what changed was that I couldn't get you out of my head." He didn't like admitting his weakness to her. But instead of feeling exposed, he felt . . . relieved and strong. "The truth is, even if I hadn't gotten Shawn's letter demanding a party, I'd have found some excuse to come back to see you."

After several seconds, Ellie glanced over her shoulder. Her eyes looked like bruised green grapes in a face as pale as the new white paint on the kitchen walls.

"It's true, Ellie. What I feel has nothing to do with this land or the dare."

She blinked.

Sam's breath caught in his chest as life returned to her eyes. She had to believe him! "I love you, Ellie. Without you, nothing matters. Not this house or the land. Nothing!" His hand lifted toward her. "I realized how I felt that morning we talked about the past, remember?"

She turned and leaned against the counter, as if her legs couldn't support her. Sam wanted to wrap her in his arms, breathe life into her, but the haunted look in her eyes held him back.

"What about the dare?"

A string of curse words escaped under his breath. Would he ever out live the family curse? That poker game had shadowed his whole life. Hands shoved in his back pockets, he glanced at the ceiling. How could he explain she meant more to him than anything this life offered? Pain throbbed behind his eyes.

"You asked if I knew what it was like to want something so bad I'd do anything to get it." He watched surprise flicker across her face. "Remember?"

Her eyes clung to his. Her voice, a rusty sound filled with emotion, said, "Yes!"

"I know that feeling far too well."

"This land, you mean?"

"Yeah." Sam held her gaze, willing her to hear him out. "It was all about the land . . . until I met you."

"Sam—"

"Please, listen!" He paced around the table. This wasn't going well. "Until I met you, all I ever wanted was to reclaim my roots."

She crossed her arms over her chest.

It was now or never. She might not believe him, but he had to try. Heart pounding, he said, "I fell in love with you the moment you started swishing the skirts of that wedding dress."

"At the wedding?"

Her face flushed with color. Her eyes started to glitter with life. Sam took his courage in his hands. "I went to New York in an attempt to recover my heritage. But there you stood, in front of hundreds of strangers, with this beautiful smile on your face as you rustled that dress around your legs, and I was lost."

"But—"

"The night before, at the bachelor party, Shawn dared me to romance the substitute bride. If I could make her fall for me, he'd give me the land." Sam threw his shoulders back and lifted his chin. Whatever she answered, he'd take it like a man. But he prayed she would realize he was telling her the truth. "You gave my life new hope. You made me laugh, and worry, but most of all, you showed me that people are what bring happiness to your life."

"Sam, I—"

"Ellie, without you," his arm lifted in a wave, "this place doesn't mean a thing. It's just a pile of timber on acres of dirt. You turned this old house into the home I dreamed it could be. You made me realize that the people you love are what's important, not possessions." His voice scraped with emotion. He took one last chance. "I love you with all my heart. Will you share the future with me?"

"Sam—"

Pain washed across her face and stabbed him in the heart. She was going to say no! "We don't have to live here. If you want, I'll move." He stopped as her head thrashed from side to side. He made one last attempt to show her how much he cared. "Just say you'll be my wife."

"I can't!" Her heart felt as if it were being ripped out. He would do that for her? He loved her! He must. Why else would he give up everything that mattered to him? But even as her heart filled with hope, her head realized the truth.

If Sam really loved her, if he meant what he said, that was all the more reason for her to leave. How could she let the man she loved make that sacrifice? She knew how much he loved this place. She would never ask him to leave it behind.

Under normal circumstances, nothing would make

her happier than to spend her life here with Sam. But her situation had never been normal.

"Can't—"

"Is it the dare?"

She could do this. She had to save Sam's future. "No, this isn't about the dare."

"Then—"

"I decided to leave before—"

Sam paced around the room. "I was afraid of that! I scared you off that night I kissed you in the bathroom."

Ellie swallowed. She could leave it there. Let him think this was his fault. But she had been taught to face facts. Dealing with the truth came naturally to her.

"You didn't scare me off," she whispered.

"Then why?"

Ellie turned away. She'd never realized hazel eyes could look like storm clouds. "It's a long story."

"I've got the time . . . my whole future."

"I don't know you well enough, Sam." She flinched at his oath. It wasn't the words she minded. It was the emotion written on his face. Ellie didn't trust emotions. "I realize that now."

"How much better do you need to know me?" Sam's words came to a halt when he saw the panic on her face. He needed to back off, quick. "You didn't ask why Shawn came—"

"Why wasn't Dawn with him?"

Sam frowned. "She's writing thank-you notes . . . or something." He shrugged. "He told me, but my mind was on other things."

"Did you get the land?"

The spark of excitement in her tone caused bands to tighten around Sam's heart. "Yeah!" A lump filled his throat. *Tell her now.*

"I'm happy for you, Sam." She grinned. "You got your dream."

His gaze dropped to the cat playing on the floor. Benny swatted a roll of ribbon along the far wall. Heaving a big sigh, he ran his hand around the back of his neck. This is where things got tricky. "Not really."

"What do you mean?" Ellie took a step closer. "That's what you wanted, isn't it?" What happened? Something was wrong. "Didn't Shawn keep his promise to sign the deed?"

"I've spent my life chasing a dream."

"Why are you using the past tense?"

"I have the land, but at what cost? It's not enough." Sam shook his head. "I focused on the wrong things." He frowned. "All this time, wasted."

"No, Sam—"

"Don't you see?" His voice rose. "I spent all this time looking back, trying to fix the past."

"Sam, I—"

"You taught me that, Ellie."

"Me?" Her voice squeaked. "What do I know?"

A grin covered his face. Feeling her insides clinch in reaction, Ellie knew why she'd tried to run away. Something about Sam touched her deepest emotions.

"You made me realize we need to live for today. You planned for the future by trying to make each day count."

"Wait!" Ellie held up a hand to stop his words. The

look on his face made her heart race. "I'm the one who's trying to make roots, remember?" Seeing the look in his eyes made her heart want to sing. Then he reached for her hand. He must love her!

"I'm trying to tell you that I'm done with living for the past." His grip tightened. "I want to live for the future." He looked in her eyes, hoping she could see into his heart. "With you."

"Sam . . ." she whispered. Pain threatened to cut her in half. She couldn't let him keep going . . . she'd never be brave enough to leave.

"I'd give it all up to be with you."

"I can't, Sam." Tears rolled down her cheeks. "I love you. But I can't marry you." She choked back the lump that threatened to block her voice. "It wouldn't be fair to you."

"Why not?" He couldn't believe what he was hearing. They were so close, yet he felt the distance starting to widen between them.

"Because . . . I don't know who I am. Don't you see?" She swallowed a sob. "I can't risk doing what my mother did." Her gaze dropped to his chin. "What if . . . what if . . ." She didn't want to say this. How could she ever look him in the eye again? "What if I ran off . . . left my family, my child . . . like my mother did?"

"Ellie—"

"I learned something from you too, Sam."

He bit back words he wanted to shout as her eyes glittered like wet emeralds. He loved her more by the moment. He couldn't let her go. Impatience and desire roughened his voice. "What?"

"I learned that roots are important, that the past counts." Ellie pulled her hands from his grip. Standing rigid, she stared up at him. "Families are important, Sam." She pressed her fingers to his lips. "I can't risk hurting you, or your future, because I don't know who I am."

Ice raced along his veins as he absorbed the finality of her tone. She meant every word. He could tell from the tilt of her chin. Her mind was made up.

"Of course the past counts," he murmured. "But the past isn't everything." When she looked away, he reached over to pull her into a loose embrace. "Ellie, think: would any of these trees be here without the past?"

Her confusion showed in the quick glance she aimed at him. Why didn't he just let her go? This hurt too much, this hashing over the same thing when there was only one answer. Still, hope grew in her heart. Shaking her head, she tried to keep her desperation from showing. "No!"

"Yet some trees die. Sometimes the roots are bad." Sam held up his hand to stop her words. "We have to cull the bad roots, and start over. Think about flowers. Have you ever transplanted an iris?"

"Yes." Her smile caused the skin on her cheeks to crinkle from dried tears. He knew she had worked with flowers with the old maid sisters. New hope clutched at her chest. "But we're not flowers, Sam. And sometimes plants don't grow because the roots are bad." She swallowed past the tears in her throat. "My parents abandoned me."

"But you never know until you try, Ellie." He pulled her hands against his chest, inching her close. "Don't you see? You don't know your past, but you know what you want for the future." He jiggled her until she gave a half-smile. "You would never abandon your child."

"How can you be so sure?" Her voice begged for reassurance. "I might have rotten roots." The whispered words begged him to be right, to prove that she had a chance.

"Look around you—look at Benny and Droopy." Desperate, Sam nodded toward the two animals watching them with intense eyes. "You love them." He stared into her eyes, daring her to disagree. "You'd never desert them. You don't have it in you." He gulped and stripped his heart bare. "Let's make a start on the future, together."

"You aren't afraid?"

Sam pulled the skeleton key out of his pocket and handed it to her. "I'm afraid of a future without you. That's why I've been carrying this key around, waiting for the right time."

"I-I don't understand."

"I want you to go with me to visit my grandparents' graves. I want to bury this key beside them as a symbol of the past. I want you to marry me."

"But I don't know who I am."

"You are the woman I love, Ellie. That's good enough for me."

"Oh, Sam!" She fell against his chest with a sob. "I love you."

His kiss melted her last doubts. The feeling of being safe returned. Sam's love was more than she'd ever dreamed possible. Her one last coherent thought as Sam's lips sealed his claim on her heart was that dreams did come true!

Epilogue

Time passed in a whirlwind of planning. The date for Shawn and Dawn's reception arrived. The day was so beautiful it took Ellie's breath away.

"Don't forget your bouquet." Stella pushed the arrangement of red and white roses into Ellie's trembling fingers. Then she turned to the chattering group in the room. "Okay, ladies, it's time to make your entrance."

Ellie followed the group of whispering, giggling women to the anteroom door. Miss Margaret was already seated on the front pew, in the space traditionally reserved for the bride's mother. Ellie's new friends stopped giggling long enough to be escorted to the row behind Miss Margaret.

Stella, the matron of honor, followed behind.

Ellie basked in the love surrounding her as she stared down the aisle of Sam's church. Twitching the skirt of

213

the wedding gown she'd made for display, she thought of her many blessings. She had friends. Her shop had more business by the day. And Sam loved her.

Handsome in a black tuxedo, he stood tall as he waited for her at the front of the church, with his best man at his side. Shawn had insisted their wedding take place on the day he'd set for Sam to throw the reception.

They had learned of Shawn's real plan the day after Sam proposed. Shawn had intended a public celebration, returning the long-sought land to Sam as the real reason for the party.

Now the celebration would serve another purpose. The Oglethorpe men would introduce their brides to their friends and neighbors in Redbud.

Ellie placed her hand in Sam's and looked into his eyes. She didn't feel nervous this time. Instead, she felt the thrill of anticipation for a future spent with the man of her dreams.

Her sassy wink met his arched look and took her back to their first meeting.

She'd thought she could follow the stand-in groom anywhere. Now Sam was her real groom, and she knew she'd made the right choice on that fateful day in New York.

With Sam, all her tomorrows would be happily ever after. She would have a real name, but all she needed was Sam's love.